"You appear to be in the wrong room."

Tilly's eyes flew open and she sat up, sending a wave of water slopping back and forth violently as she drew in a sharp breath.

"Dexter!" Glad of the thick layer of jasmine bubbles, which came up to her neck, she nevertheless instinctively drew her knees in toward her, hugging them to her chest. Deep blue eyes bored into her, his expression unreadable...calm, assured and impassive, as usual giving nothing away.

"What the hell are you doing here?" She glanced at the shocking-pink bra and underwear she'd left strewn on the floor inches from his feet and willed him not to notice them.

"I could ask you the same question."

"This is *my* room."

"This is room five."

How can he just stand there, impassive, with my shocking-pink underwear at his feet and me naked in the bath? But his lips had parted just slightly, and for a second his gaze strayed from her eyes to her mouth, and he drew in a breath. Perhaps he couldn't mask everything he felt.

Dear Reader,

Thank you for picking up a copy of *Wedding Fling to Forever,* which is set in the emergency department of Trafalgar Hospital in London and in a castle on the wild and beautiful coast of Northumbria in the far northeast of England.

I visit this beautiful part of the world as much as I can and have often thought of having it as a backdrop to a romance—its wild, rugged beauty is perfect as the setting for a love story.

The love story I chose to take place there is between cool, buttoned-up A&E consultant Dexter and cancer survivor and ray of sunshine Tilly, a nurse who has brought warmth, joy and fun into the department, leaving Dexter completely at a loss for how to deal with her.

Being forced to share a room at a wedding in the medieval castle on the cliff top overlooking miles of sandy beach and the wild North Sea might just allow Tilly to tease Dexter into loosening up and enjoying what life has to offer...if only he can go against his self-imposed rules and allow himself to feel again.

I do hope you enjoy it.

Colette X

WEDDING FLING TO FOREVER

COLETTE COOPER

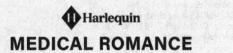

MEDICAL ROMANCE

If you purchased this book without a cover you should be aware that this book is stolen property. It was reported as "unsold and destroyed" to the publisher, and neither the author nor the publisher has received any payment for this "stripped book."

Harlequin®
MEDICAL ROMANCE

Recycling programs for this product may not exist in your area.

ISBN-13: 978-1-335-99322-9

Wedding Fling to Forever

Copyright © 2025 by Colette Cooper

All rights reserved. No part of this book may be used or reproduced in any manner whatsoever without written permission.

Without limiting the author's and publisher's exclusive rights, any unauthorized use of this publication to train generative artificial intelligence (AI) technologies is expressly prohibited.

This is a work of fiction. Names, characters, places and incidents are either the product of the author's imagination or are used fictitiously. Any resemblance to actual persons, living or dead, businesses, companies, events or locales is entirely coincidental.

For questions and comments about the quality of this book, please contact us at CustomerService@Harlequin.com.

TM and ® are trademarks of Harlequin Enterprises ULC.

Harlequin Enterprises ULC
22 Adelaide St. West, 41st Floor
Toronto, Ontario M5H 4E3, Canada
www.Harlequin.com

Printed in U.S.A.

Reading the Ladybird book *The Nurse* as a child sowed the seeds for **Colette Cooper's** future career. Using her experiences as a nurse to write medical romances with vibrant, interesting heroes and heroines to fall in love with is a dream come true. Colette lives in a beach house in Australia in her daydreams, but in reality, she lives in the Heart of England, just about as far from the sea as it is possible to be in the UK but very close to the home of Mr. Fitzwilliam Darcy! As well as writing, she practices yoga, which she isn't bad at, and French, which needs much more practice!

Books by Colette Cooper

Nurse's Twin Baby Surprise

Visit the Author Profile page at Harlequin.com.

For my dad, who instilled in me a love of
books and storytelling.

**Praise for
Colette Cooper**

"Fabulous. This is exactly what I want from my
Mills and Boon stories... This debut novel from
Colette Cooper is so good and I am really looking
forward to reading her next book."

—*Goodreads* on
Nurse's Twin Baby Surprise

CHAPTER ONE

'HELICOPTER INBOUND. ETA five minutes. Thirty-two-year-old male patient. Car versus bicycle. Multiple injuries including head, chest and pelvis. Peri arrest.'

Though calm and measured, Sister Tilly Clover's voice immediately had everyone's attention, and the team in the vicinity of the red trauma-phone in London's Trafalgar Hospital's resus room turned to look at her and await instructions.

The patient heading towards them was going to require every single member of the team to give the best they had—he was peri arrest, on the verge of his heart stopping altogether, which was as bad as it got. She knew full well that what she said next could affect the outcome for the patient they were expecting and having the shrewd, dark eyes of consultant Dexter Stevens surveying her as she spoke did nothing to quell the sudden banging of her heart against her ribs.

'Mark and Hannah, come with me to Resus, please. Ally, can you bleep the ortho and neuro registrars? Anika, run a unit through the blood warmer at four. I'll bleep the radiographer.'

How many times she'd done a similar call to arms, she couldn't begin to remember, but every time the thought that someone's life had just changed, might even end, sent a shot of unwelcome yet rousing adrenaline surging through her veins. This was why she loved her job so much. Dealing with situations like this was second nature, and knowing she could make a difference to someone's life was so incredibly rewarding. The fact that she'd come so close to death herself just a few short years ago was a constant reminder of the vital role that highly trained, caring professionals had in people's lives—but also of the fact that life could be taken away so easily and so randomly.

'I'll take this.'

Dexter Stevens' commanding tone told her he didn't expect her to challenge him, and she wasn't about to surprise him by doing so. The lead A&E consultant, with his smouldering eyes, hard-edged cheekbones and ability to look disarmingly dashing even in hospital scrubs, was the best option the patient being air-lifted towards them as they spoke was going to get. The problem was, he knew it.

'He'll be in four,' said Tilly.

'I heard,' he replied. 'And?'

Tilly knew what he meant. Dexter Stevens was a man of few words and those he did speak were precise, to the point and always brusque. 'Witnesses say the cyclist was hit from behind at around forty miles per hour. He has multiple injuries including head, chest and pelvis; possible spinal injuries; immediate loss of consciousness, and was peri-arrest after being scooped by the heli medics. He's already intubated and on a portable ventilator.'

'Impossible to tell from that whether his biggest problem is brain injury or blood loss,' he replied, slipping the 'Team Leader' tabard on over his scrubs.

How could he make that sound as though it was her fault?

'Quite,' she replied, flicking the switch to turn on the monitor, its coloured lines flashing to life on the screen. 'I suppose it's our job to find out.'

'It's that of the CT scanners, to be precise.' He checked his watch.

Tilly rolled her eyes. He was so literal. 'And there's me thinking we had a useful role to play.' She grinned at him, but the tiniest twitch of his dark eyebrows drawing inwards and the slight confusion in his intense blue eyes told her that her quip had flown completely over his dark, stormy head.

Those eyes, a piercing cobalt blue, seemed to bore into her soul and see her innermost secrets and thoughts. Hopefully not—for, if they could, they'd see that she wanted to gaze into them, melt into his strong arms and kiss lips that, though they were rarely seen to smile, were nevertheless entirely kissable.

She swallowed hard, unsure whether it was the incident they were about to have to deal with or Dexter Stevens' dark gaze that was the cause of the adrenaline suddenly coursing through her veins. What she did know was that she was grateful that the consultant striding away from her with such purposeful, feral grace was here right now and would give this desperately ill patient the very best chance he had of surviving the extreme trauma he'd suffered.

The doors to Resus crashed open as the helicopter medics rushed in with their patient. The calm before the storm was over.

'Okay, team,' said Dexter, looking suddenly more at home. 'This is a category one trauma—a proper cat one. Let's go. Airway?' He stood at the patient's side, addressing the helicopter medic, taking control, calm, assured, poised and dominating the scene.

'Intubated and patent,' replied the heli medic.

Dexter fired orders, which everyone immediately and swiftly obeyed. 'Ally, put in an arterial line and take bloods, including a cross-match for ten units. Mark, obs. Hannah, direct pressure to the left thigh wound. Anika, run the O-neg through stat and have the next ready. Tilly, check pelvis for stability. Questions, anyone?'

'BP eighty over forty,' called Mark, one of the nurse practitioners. 'Heart rate, one twenty and temperature is thirty-five.'

'Instigate the MHP,' said Dexter. 'We need to stabilise him as much as possible; get him into the CT scanner and see fully what we're dealing with here. I suspect he has massive internal bleeding from the pelvis and possibly intra-abdominally too.'

The MHP, or massive haemorrhage protocol, was only instigated for life-threatening blood loss to carefully manage the need for rapid transfusion support. Dexter had recognised the need immediately and was swiftly coordinating the actions of the team to maximise this patient's chances. Literally every second counted. The man lying battered, bruised, broken and bleeding on the trolley before them had a limited chance of getting through this, but he was being given the best chance possible because Dexter Stevens had decided to take control.

Inspecting the pelvic binder that had been applied by the paramedics, Tilly knew Dexter's eyes were on her. She could feel the power they exerted, burning into her, scrutinising her every move, assessing, judging. This patient was a category one trauma—the worst there was—and Dexter was in his element. He was completely at home, ensuring that every single member of the team pulled their weight to give the patient every chance there was to survive this. Somehow, he had the ability to bring out the best in the team when it really mattered... and Tilly hadn't yet quite worked out exactly how he did it.

'How's he doing at the head end?' asked Dexter. The trauma team-leader had overall control of the situation without being bogged down in performing any of the individual tasks the rest of the team carried out and, as far as Tilly was concerned, Dexter was one of the best she'd ever seen. It was an extraordinarily stressful position, but he was able to perform in the most difficult circumstances with the utmost competence and calm professionalism. He also managed to do it with an undisputable and impressive authority that, much to her increasing despair, Tilly found achingly attractive.

'Oxygen sats ninety-six; good air entry,' replied Trent, the heli-medic.

'Pelvis?' said Dexter, turning his attention to Tilly.

'Pelvis unstable; belt in situ,' she replied. 'Abdomen distended and firm, indicating bleeding.'

'Check if CT are ready. We'll need a full body scan to find out what's going on in there.'

'Sure,' she replied, stepping away and lifting the phone to call CT.

Why did the way he'd looked at her make her heart bang even harder in her chest?

It had happened the very first time he'd locked his eyes on hers four months ago, when she'd started her job at Trafalgar Hospital, and every time since. But Dexter Stevens was the last man on earth she should get involved with. If she was going to get involved with anyone ever again, she wanted someone steady, reliable and sensible. Someone who wouldn't flee like a scalded cat when he found out about her leukaemia. Someone who'd genuinely care about her, who would be there if things got tough again and would stick around even if she wasn't always the life and soul of the party. In short, someone who wasn't in the least like her ex, Lachlan.

Her jaw clenched. She was over him…way over him. But he had left a mark. She should be grateful to him, really. He'd taught her a lesson: steer well clear of men who were only interested in having a good time; hold out for someone who genuinely cared about her, who would be reliable through good times and bad; and definitely don't be so easily seduced by handsome good looks.

No. Safe, steady and reliable were the absolute prerequisites for giving her heart away again.

And Dexter was none of those things. Darkly luscious, always composed, he had a brooding charisma, which meant that, although everyone in the department held him in the highest esteem, no one really seemed to know anything about him. He didn't socialise with the team, nor did he have any friendships within the department.

He was a lone wolf, neither welcoming nor seeking friendship from anyone. He never went for a coffee or drink after work, and never entered into any conversations about anything other than what he needed to about patients. He was Head of Department but was the one person everyone knew the least about. Which meant he was the last person she should spend so much time thinking about.

She returned to the cubicle. 'CT scanner is ready whenever we are.'

'Excellent.' This time he didn't floor her with his penetrating gaze but glanced at Mark. 'Obs?'

'BP ninety-five over fifty; heart-rate ninety.'

'Better,' replied Dexter. 'GCS is still nine. Let's get him into CT. Trent, stay at the head; Tilly, you come along too.'

Tilly loaded all the portable monitoring equipment onto the bed alongside their patient. It turned out he was a thirty-two-year-old teacher called Martin Cookson who had simply been out for a leisurely bike ride along the country lanes near his home when a car had ploughed into the back of him, throwing him into the air and causing him to land heavily on the road. Luckily, the friend who'd been riding with him was a junior doctor who'd recognised the need for an air ambulance and had been able to give first aid.

The control room in the scanner suite was necessarily darkened. The only light came from the bank of monitors that glowed with images of scanned slices through Martin's body which Dexter was examining silently. The small room hadn't been designed to provide much in the way of appropriate personal space, and somehow she'd ended up with him on her left and the wall on her right. She leant against the cool wall, pressing herself into it just to try to create a little space between them. The thought of accidentally brushing against him sent a delicious shudder through her spine but she knew that, if she did brush his skin with her own, he would once again be the last thing she thought about before she fell asleep that night. It was already happening all too often lately.

'Subdural bleed in the left occipital region in keeping with the abrasion on the head,' remarked Dexter, his focus on the CT scanner screen, which was whirring and beeping its way methodically down Martin's battered body. 'Cervical spine intact; left-sided haemothorax as expected.'

He stood, hands casually in the pockets of his navy scrubs, legs apart, dark head bent slightly as he gazed at the mesmerising, ever-changing images on the screen. He could have been a movie star, he was so damn handsome.

Was that why she was so drawn to him? Because of his perfect good looks, toned body and smouldering, 'come to bed' eyes?

Hell, no. Someone that good-looking was surely not to be trusted. Was it because she admired his incomparable ability as an A&E doctor? There was no doubt she did admire that, but she'd worked with plenty of excellent medical staff before and not found herself drifting off to sleep at night thinking about them.

'Vital signs holding,' she advised.

Dexter continued his running commentary.

'Thoracic spine clear.' But then his eyes narrowed. 'There's one culprit. He has a splenic tear—grade five.'

Tilly's heart sank. Grade five was the most severe and suddenly Martin's life was in even greater and more imminent danger.

'Hi, what have we got?' Robert Luscombe, general surgeon, strode in.

'Cyclist versus car,' replied Dexter, still studying the screen. 'Forty miles an hour; minor subdural bleed; treated haemothorax; grade five splenic injury and…there we go. A fractured pelvis with significant bleeding. This is going to take some sorting out.'

His expression was impassive. He was just stating a fact—a cold, hard fact. Tilly's heart went out

16 WEDDING FLING TO FOREVER

to the young man who'd simply been enjoying the fresh air on a summer's day and now lay with his life held in that fragile place between life and death, completely in the hands of the medical team around him. But Dexter Stevens, once again, was emotionless. In the four months she'd worked at this prestigious major trauma centre in the heart of London, she'd never seen a shred of emotion from him—not under any circumstances. Nothing ever touched him.

'Have the orthos answered yet?' Dexter asked, moving away from the screen, having apparently seen everything he needed to.

'On their way,' replied Tilly.

'We'll have to work with the orthos on him at the same time,' said Robert, grimacing. 'He's in a bad way, poor guy. I'll get into Theatre now, so send him straight from here if you like.'

'Will do,' said Dexter, opening the door. 'Let's go.'

Tilly glanced at him, her stomach doing a silly somersault as she briefly caught his eye, before slipping back into the scanner room to ready the patient for transfer.

Why on earth did she find him so fascinating?

It made no sense. Instinctively she knew she shouldn't go within a million miles of him, but something about him drew her in. It was more than unnerving. Dexter Stevens was an untouchable, cool operator with a heart of ice, and every fibre of her being told her to stay well away from him. The problem was, although her head logically told her that, it only seemed to make him all the more interesting.

His exceptionally quick, analytical thinking was highly impressive and had served him well in stabilising their seriously ill patient, diagnosing his injuries and instigating treatment. But if he cared about poor Martin Cookson, he didn't let it show. Not one bit. And that should be a red flag—a big red flag—waving in the breeze as a warning to stop wondering what it would be like to be held in his strong, toned arms. But, for some unfathomable reason, the red flag didn't shout a warning to Tilly, it beckoned her, tempting her, luring her towards him. For, if there was one thing her brush with her own mortality had taught her, it was that she wanted to live.

Tilly Clover bothered him…much more than he cared to admit. He glanced at her sideways as he wrote in his patient's notes. She'd scooped up a crying toddler with bloody knees and a bleeding head wound, said something in his ear and made him stop crying in seconds. The child was now safely ensconced on an examination couch and Tilly was playing some game with a teddy bear, making the now calm and happy toddler chuckle with delight.

Was she a child whisperer or something? Why couldn't he do that?

'Dr Stevens?'

He swung round, startled, hoping he hadn't been clocked looking at Tilly. It was Pearl, one of the junior doctors, and she was smiling.

18 WEDDING FLING TO FOREVER

'I've just had a call from ITU—Martin Cookson, the cyclist from this morning, is out of Theatre. It's good news—they managed to do an open reduction and internal fixation on the pelvis, and the splenectomy was successful.'

He nodded. 'Can you see the patient in Majors, bed five, please, Dr Giles?' he replied, aware her eyebrows had drawn together very slightly at his response.

'I just thought you'd want to know.' She turned and left, heading towards Majors.

It was good news that their earlier patient was now much more stable, but there were currently scores of other people in the department who needed to be seen, and his policy had always been that once a patient left A&E he tried not to think further about them. That was how he rolled. Caring too much about everyone who came through the doors would be a sure-fire way to burn out faster than a cheetah could chase down a tortoise. Remaining detached was far preferable and had served him well all his professional life—most of his life, full stop. Living with a grieving, angry, alcoholic father had taught him many things, one of which was that emotions and caring about people only got him hurt...in more ways than one.

'Dexter, can you have a look at a three-year-old in seven, please?'

Tilly. Sister Tilly Clover. He'd know that sunshine voice of hers anywhere, even with his eyes shut. Whoever had recruited her into his department four months ago hadn't realised just how much of an effect her presence would bring—both to A&E and, disconcertingly, to himself. It wouldn't be an exaggeration to say that, although she'd brought with her first-class nursing skills, she'd also brought what he could only describe as the brightest and most annoying sparkle he'd ever seen. She hummed everywhere she went, and when she wasn't humming she was singing. Everyone had immediately taken to her as though she'd sprinkled magic fairy-dust on them…

Everyone except him. According to everyone else, she was one of the wonders of the world and had breathed fresh air, light and energy into the department. But, as far as he was concerned, the department had been fine as it was. Tilly Clover was an excellent nurse, there was no question of that. But she hadn't arrived quietly and apprehensively, as new members of staff usually did; she'd arrived with a flourish, a penchant for fun and a quick wit, which she far too regularly directed at him. And he didn't know how to respond.

'What's the problem?'

'James: three years old; bright as a button yesterday but this morning was difficult to rouse from sleep. Temp thirty-nine point five; resps forty-five; fretful but drowsy. I've checked him for a rash and there's nothing, but his hands and feet are pretty cold. I'm concerned it could be meningitis. Would you take a look at him, please?'

If Tilly was concerned about a patient, then so

was he. She wasn't one to worry for no reason. 'Any other symptoms? Aversion to light? Vomiting?'

'No. It could just be a simple viral infection, but the cold extremities are a bit of a red flag, and I want you to cast your eyes over him. Better safe than sorry.' She pulled back the curtain to the cubicle and addressed James's mum, Emma Carpenter, who was cradling him. 'This is Dr Stevens.'

'Sister Clover has asked me to take a look at your son.'

'Of course, Doctor. On the couch?'

'He's fine there,' said Dexter. The boy was white as a sheet and clearly febrile. He barely registered as Dexter examined him, carefully checking every inch of his skin, gently turning him to look at his back and finding a small but telling rash. Tilly had been right to be concerned. He needed to get a lumbar puncture done and a specimen sent to the lab asap.

'Sister, can you set up for an LP and ask one of the staff to draw up the antibiotics IV? I'll get a line in and take bloods.'

'What's an LP?' asked James's mum, her gaze darting from her son to Dexter.

'A lumbar puncture,' he replied. And the pressure to get it done was immense.

'That rash has appeared in the last few minutes,' said Tilly, her startlingly unusual amethyst eyes full of concern. 'I did check.'

'The trolley, please,' replied Dexter. Time was of the essence. There was no time to reassure Tilly that he was sure she'd checked or to remind her of what she likely already knew—that a meningitis rash could be absent one minute and present the next.

'Is he going to be all right, Doctor?' Emma Carpenter's eyes were wide.

'We need to do the tests to be sure, Mrs Carpenter,' he replied. 'Can you place James on the couch, please, on his side?'

'Try not to worry, Emma,' said Tilly, touching the woman's arm lightly. 'You did the right thing, bringing James in, which means we can do the tests and start treatment nice and early. Mother's intuition is a wonderful thing.'

She smiled, drawing the curtains aside, calling to one of the other staff to get the antibiotic. She'd registered the seriousness of the situation; he'd seen it in her eyes when he'd uncovered the rash. Those extraordinary eyes...always sparkling with joy, fun and laughter. He'd learned very quickly that they only lost their sparkle when she was truly worried. And right now, quite rightly, they were full of concern.

'Just going to insert a cannula, Mrs Carpenter.'

'What's that for?' she asked, still looking terrified. As ever, difficult as it was, Dexter tried not to look into her eyes, at least not for longer than he had to. Getting involved emotionally with patients was never a good thing. Remaining detached, keeping a cool head, was far better for everyone involved.

'I need to take some bloods, and we'll use it to give fluids and any drugs too.'

'Do you want me to run saline through that?' asked Tilly, reappearing with the silver trolley.

'Yes,' he replied, thankful she hadn't taken long. This little boy was in a bad way. Every minute they delayed could be the difference between him living to recover completely, being left with a lifelong disability or not making it at all. His mum planted a tender kiss on the top of his head, still cradling him, and for a moment Dexter watched the way she looked at her son, her eyes full of both love and fear for the little boy.

Tilly had been correct; Emma Carpenter had been right to bring her son into hospital as quickly as she had. He never underestimated a mother's intuition when it came to knowing her child. Would his own mother have been the same with him...if she'd lived? He'd never know but, growing up, he'd always liked to think that she would have loved him, as this mother clearly loved little James.

'I'll gown up,' he said, dismissing the thought. It was no good thinking like that—that wasn't going to help James or his mum.

He snapped on the sterile gloves as Tilly tied the back of the gown behind him. Blue sterile drapes in place, Dexter carefully located the exact point of entry for the spinal needle, inserting it swiftly and aspirating the clear spinal fluid that would tell them if, as suspected, James had bacterial meningitis. The effect of the adrenaline surging through his veins was difficult to ignore. This procedure was intricate and carried grave risks.

It would be easy to acknowledge the way his heart rate had ratchetted up and put it down to the fact that he cared. But caring alone wasn't going to help James and his family, was it? What they needed right now was someone who was competent, could think clearly and get this diagnosis and treatment right. Caring didn't come into it. Caring was best left to people like Tilly—people who seemed to know what to do with feelings like that.

'Ready for the dressing?' asked Tilly.

He moved his hand in answer to her question and she reached in, brushing his arm as she smoothed the dressing down and leant in to whisper in James's ear.

'All done, James. You did really well. Stay lying down there and Mummy will read you a story.'

She smiled at his mum, her eyes full of sparkle, again and his stomach clenched. And, not for the first time in the last four months, Dexter Stevens was worried. Finding a woman physically attractive was one thing but, with those exquisite amethyst eyes, glossy dark hair highlighted with subtle wisps of the same colour and vivacious ability to make everyone smile when she entered the room, Tilly Clover was something else.

He drew in a breath. *Stop it.* He admired her abilities as a first-class nurse—end of. That was all.

'What happens now?' asked James's mum, stroking her son's blond head but with her gaze still firmly fixed on Dexter.

'We give the antibiotics,' he replied, 'and wait

24   WEDDING FLING TO FOREVER

for the LP results.' He pulled the gown, tearing the paper ties and scrunching it into a ball before placing it into a bin. He wished he could say more, wished he could tell her that little James was going to be fine, but no one knew that yet, and he wasn't going to give false hope. Being disappointed over something that meant everything was devastating. He'd learned that lesson many times over.

'But he's going to be okay, isn't he? Doctor…?' Emma Carpenter's gaze flicked from him to Tilly and back again. 'Please tell me he's going to be okay.'

Her eyes were wide and glossy with quickly forming tears. His stomach sank. His training and experience meant that he knew exactly what to do for a sick child—piece together the puzzle of diagnosis by assessing the signs and symptoms, quickly formulate and instigate the correct treatment plan then rapidly and expertly perform the required procedures. What he was less able to do was provide Emma Carpenter with the cast-iron reassurance she wanted, because that would mean letting go of the strict rules he lived by.

'I'm popping the antibiotics in now,' said Tilly, throwing him a quizzical look as she attached an IV line to the cannula in James's arm. 'Which means they'll get working to fight the infection straight away. He's in the best place, Emma, and you did well to bring him in so quickly. It's a matter of keeping everything crossed now—and, more importantly, for you to read that book to James.' She smiled. It was a warm, genuine smile and Emma Carpenter managed a smile back before picking up the story book and turning her attention back to her son.

How did Tilly do that? How did she know exactly the right thing to say? And why didn't he? It was because the strict rules Dexter lived by didn't include giving the sort of things that Tilly could provide. In order to provide the high level of expertise he strived to achieve, he needed to remain professional at all times. And that meant becoming emotionally involved with patients and their lives wasn't advisable. Emotions muddied the waters, muddled clear thinking and confused logic. He was a better doctor for being able to see and think clearly without the distraction of sentiment.

'All done,' whispered Tilly, smiling at Emma, who smiled back, continuing to read out loud to James. 'See you in a bit.' Emma nodded as Tilly pulled the curtain to one side.

'I'll give the lab an hour,' said Dexter as they left the cubicle. 'And if we haven't heard anything I'll give them a call for the results.'

'Do you think he'll be okay?' asked Tilly, tapping on a tablet to sign for the antibiotics.

'Hopefully,' replied Dexter. 'It looks as though it's been caught early. The rash appeared practically before our eyes and we got the antibiotics in quickly.'

'Perhaps it would help Emma if you told her that.' She glanced up at him, her lips pressed together and one dark eyebrow raised.

'I don't want to give her false hope. I'll give her more information when I have it.'

26   WEDDING FLING TO FOREVER

Tilly drew in a breath. 'It's not really *false* hope, though, is it? It's *actual* hope. I think sometimes, it's good to give that—patients need hope. Try it some time.' She picked up a phone at the nurse's station and dialled a number.

Dexter blinked. *Had she just had a go at him?* He sat down and logged into a computer. He'd just done a damn good job. He'd made a diagnosis and initiated the correct treatment efficiently and effectively. He'd done what he'd trained hard to do but Tilly Clover seemed to think that his medical expertise wasn't complete because he hadn't offered empty promises to a concerned mum.

He opened James notes and updated them with the facts, and not with false platitudes. He was good at his job, and no one was going to tell him differently.

One of the reasons he'd wanted to become a doctor so badly, despite the obstacles which had lain in his path, was to give something back. One of the few times he'd ever felt he mattered to anyone had been as a young child, when he'd been admitted to A&E himself with appendicitis. He'd seen how flawlessly professional the doctors and nurses had been—how swiftly they'd acted, how calmly they'd performed what they'd needed to and how grateful he'd been that they'd taken over from the chaos that had been his drunken father.

He'd been so determined to study medicine that even his father telling him that the idea was preposterous, and that he should get over himself with his grand ideas, hadn't deterred him. Neither had the fact that he didn't exactly come from the sort of background that medical students usually came from. He hadn't been able to afford extra tuition to pass the entrance exams or the books to study from. Even earning enough money to scrape together enough for the train fare to go to university open days and for interviews had required him to work long hours in the evenings and weekends in a supermarket warehouse. And he'd done it. He'd passed the exams to be awarded a scholarship to study medicine at Oxford and graduated with first class honours.

But he'd never rested on his laurels—he wanted to be the best A&E consultant. He wanted to be able to give other people the same level of care he'd received as a frightened child when his father had been escorted down to the café to sober up and the staff left around him had, for the first time in his life, made him feel that he mattered. Their professionalism, their attention to detail and their expertise was what had saved his life. He'd never admired anyone until that point. But suddenly he'd found his purpose, and he couldn't thank them enough for providing it.

He'd achieved what he'd set out to achieve. He was a consultant in one of the most prestigious emergency departments in the country. Every day, he made good decisions; every day, he made a difference to people's lives—and he didn't need Tilly Clover pointing out that doing all that wasn't quite good enough.

28 WEDDING FLING TO FOREVER

He didn't need that because he already knew. He was a good doctor but he had rules. Rules that Tilly Clover wouldn't understand: Keep a professional distance.

Don't let emotions get in the way of logical decision making.

Dexter Stevens didn't do feelings—in fact, he'd spent almost his whole life avoiding them with patients and everyone else. It had worked for him... mostly.

Helena had been the exception. He'd allowed feelings in then. Or thought he had. Apparently, he hadn't let them in enough and she'd found someone else. He'd tried to erase the words she'd shouted at him when he'd seen her new lover leave through the back door of her house as he'd come in the front.

Someone who doesn't have a heart of unbreakable steel... Someone who can tell me he loves me...

He'd thought he had shown her he loved her. He'd never told her, though. And it hadn't been enough.

His heart wasn't made of unbreakable steel. It had shattered. And he was never going to risk it shattering again.

Which meant sticking to his rules. Emotions and feelings were Tilly's forte, not his. He had no need of them. He could function better without them. Emotions only complicated life, and were to be avoided at all costs, because he'd known for a long time that feeling something would end the world as he knew it.

CHAPTER TWO

ANIKA, ONE OF the nurses, sank down into a chair at the nurse's station beside Tilly with an exhausted sigh.

'You okay?' said Tilly, looking up. 'Anything I can help with?'

'Dexter dealt with it,' replied Anika. 'In his usual affable way. I'd put a couple of sutures in this patient's eyebrow...disagreement in the pub as per... and he started kicking off about his wait time. Anyway, Dexter must have heard, came in and read him the riot act in that cool-as-a-cucumber way he has that somehow shuts people up in a second.'

'Go and get a coffee,' said Tilly. 'I'm almost finished here, so I can crack on with the next patient. You deserve a quick break.' The job was challenging enough without having to take abuse, and staff needed to support each other when that happened.

'You sure?'

'Absolutely. Go, go!' Tilly smiled and waved her away like a mother hen, just as Dexter came round the corner and walked towards them.

'Ah, Anika,' he said. 'Have you finished in cubicle twelve? I need it for a patient.'

Anika brought her palm to her forehead. 'Oh, sorry—I haven't cleared away, have I?'

'I'll do it,' said Tilly, 'if you can run that errand for me...please?'

'Oh...the errand...yes. Thanks, Tilly.' Anika gave Dexter a weak smile and left.

'She's thanking you for getting her to run an *errand*?' said Dexter, a dark eyebrow raised above the bluest eyes. Tilly's stomach flipped.

'She's very polite,' replied Tilly, turning back to the computer, reluctant to look away from him but hoping that by doing so her heart rate might return to normal. It didn't. 'I hear you just booted a lively patient out of the department.'

He sat down and logged onto the computer, his nearness making her breathing deepen as always. 'Not booted, no. I merely explained that I was giving him the opportunity to leave quietly. He very wisely took the advice.'

'I don't know how you do it, Dexter—you have the knack of being able to persuade people like that guy to behave. Security love it—you do their job for them.' She logged out of her own machine and swivelled her chair to get up.

'Good to know I have your approval on that at least, Sister,' he replied. 'Anyway, there's no need for heavy handedness.'

'It's the only language some people understand, though, isn't it?' He was referring to her remark earlier about reassuring James's mum. Dexter wasn't completely beyond reproach, especially when it came to his communication skills.

'There's nothing that can't be solved with the right words,' he replied.

'And yet, you're a man of so few.' She smiled at

him, slotted her pen back into her pocket and headed for cubicle twelve. In her first four months at Trafalgar Hospital, Tilly had got the lowdown on every single member of staff, from cleaners to consultants. She knew their names, their partners' and children's names and, most importantly, how they liked their tea. But Dexter Stevens was a closed book. No, not just closed... He was like one of those secret diaries she'd had as a teen, with a great big padlock and key hidden away where no one could find it.

And that was what pulled her towards him. That and those piercing blue eyes, not to mention the ripped body and glossy raven hair that flopped casually over one eye when he dipped his head at a certain angle.

'Cubicle twelve,' he called after her.

She didn't turn round but raised her hand in acknowledgement as she continued to walk away from him. Dexter Stevens might well be in possession of a body that could only be described as perfection, and eyes she could lose herself in for days, but although the pull of him was powerful she was determined to resist. Dexter Stevens was a delicious temptation but the dark, mysterious air he pulled around himself like a cloak was a warning to stay back.

She cleared the cubicle quickly.

'Ready?' Dexter peered round the curtain.

'All done,' she replied. He'd given her all of one and a half minutes.

'I'll get the next patient.'

'Oh, before you go...did you get James's results?'

'As expected,' he replied. 'Bacterial meningitis.'

'Have you spoken to his mum?'

'Not yet.'

'I'll come with you, after this.'

'I'm quite capable of—' he began.

'I know,' butted in Tilly. 'But she was super-worried and she'll probably be upset.'

Dexter looked back at her, a slight frown creasing his brow.

'She'll need an explanation and a bit of support,' clarified Tilly.

His frown deepened.

'And we all know that's not where your particular strengths lie, Dr Stevens.'

His eyebrows nearly reached his hairline. Tilly held up her hands. 'I'm just saying,' she continued, 'that your strengths lie more in your practical skills rather than in...you know...being nice to people.'

'That's not true.'

She pursed her lips, folding her arms. 'Let's just say, there's room for improvement.'

'Knock, knock,' came a female voice from the other side of the curtain.

'Come in,' said Tilly.

The curtain inched open. It was Geetha Iyengar, the hospital's chief executive.

'Ah, here you are, Dexter—tracked you down at last.'

'Can I help?' he replied.

'I don't want to bother you if you're busy; have you got a moment?'

Dexter looked pointedly behind the CEO to the overflowing waiting area, saying nothing. He didn't need to. Geetha turned to look, took a moment and returned her gaze to meet Dexter's cool, questioning stare.

'I think I'm still missing your RSVP,' she said, her hands clasped in front of her.

'Think?' he replied.

'I *am* missing it,' she clarified. 'Unless you've posted it in the last couple of days?'

'I haven't.'

She sighed. 'Then can you, please? The hotel needs numbers and it's only two weeks away now.'

'I bet you can't wait,' said Tilly. 'Two weeks until your wedding. It sounds amazing. I'm looking forward to the banana-leaf meal.'

'I'm so glad you're coming, Tilly, and thanks for your RSVP. It's just you, isn't it? No plus one?'

'Just me,' she replied with a smile.

Dexter once again looked pointedly behind Geetha to the full waiting room. 'We should probably get on.'

Tilly couldn't help but roll her eyes at Geetha, whose gaze darted back to Dexter, who was checking his watch.

'If a verbal RSVP is adequate, I accept your invitation,' said Dexter. 'Now, we really should see some patients.'

Tilly blinked slowly. *Had he really just spoken to lovely Geetha as though she were the hospital cat? And had he actually meant it to sound as though,*

34

WEDDING FLING TO FOREVER

by accepting her kind wedding invitation, he'd done her a favour?

'Thank you, Dexter—will there be a plus one?'

'No,' he replied.

'I'll leave you to get on, then. I have a meeting with Finance this afternoon to discuss the possibility of purchasing the new ENT equipment you requested. I'll let you know how it goes at some point…when you have time.'

Tilly smiled gleefully at the CEO's punchy parting shot, Dexter's scowl as he watched Geetha leave only widening her smile further. Well, he shouldn't have been so rude.

'See?' said Tilly, nodding towards the curtain. 'Room for improvement.'

'No one's suggested that before, but thank you for your advice.'

'You're welcome.' She beamed.

'I'm going to get the next patient,' he said, arching an eyebrow.

She gave a mock salute, making his eyebrow rise further. He walked past her, his earthy, warm, masculine scent filling her nostrils as he breezed out. She took a deep breath, breathing in more of him, aware her heart was beating a little harder and faster, as it did every time her attraction towards him reached her awareness…as it did far too often. She threw the wipes into the bin and pulled down a fresh sheet of paper roll to cover the couch, glancing round the cubicle and making sure everything was in order.

It was—much more in order than her head, which currently seemed to be controlled by two conflicting creatures: a sensible fairy godmother who reminded her that Dexter Stevens, with his surly manner and sarcastic quips, was the absolute opposite of the kind, caring, thoughtful man she wanted; and an annoying, prodding imp who made her wonder what the contours of the muscles beneath his navy scrubs would feel like under her fingers. When he wasn't near, the voice of the fairy godmother was louder, but in his presence the imp shouted loudest and was becoming impossible to ignore.

She wanted adventure, didn't she? Throughout the years of chemo, dreaming of the adventures she might have one day was what had kept her going, kept her fighting. Becoming a nurse, leaving home, going to work in London were all things she'd dreamt of when life itself had been hanging in the balance. Leukaemia had almost claimed her life, but it had also given her dreams, and now she was determined to live them. That was what going to work in Australia was all about—finding the biggest challenge, the greatest test, the ultimate dream.

Not knowing how long she had left to live had focussed her mind. And Tilly's mind had focussed over and over again on the same thing: an adventure that had started as a tiny nugget of an idea one night when she hadn't been able to sleep because of the exquisitely painful mouth ulcers she'd developed during the second round of chemo. A nurse had done

WEDDING FLING TO FOREVER

a session of guided imagery with her and she'd tried to imagine herself on a wide, sandy beach, soaking up the warm rays of the sun, picking up a handful of warm sand and letting it run through her fingers as she listened to the waves lapping softly a few feet away.

She'd imagined the beach was in Australia and the rest was history. A plan had taken shape, online research had been done and an adventure had emerged bit by bit that she'd clung onto through every subsequent round of chemo. It had been the best therapy. It had sustained her through two years of active treatment and through the draining tiredness, the unrelenting nausea, the weight loss and the infections.

And the smothering love from her family. She could only imagine the hell her family had gone through when she'd been diagnosed aged thirteen and when she'd gone through the rounds of gruelling chemo. Naturally, they'd wanted to protect her—she understood that—but being wrapped in cotton wool so tightly had become stifling. As her friends had planned their careers and trips abroad, got boyfriends and planned their futures, she hadn't even known if she would have a future. Everyone around her, well-meaning as they absolutely were, had only confirmed that in the way they'd protected her so fervently. She'd longed to be free from the constraints her well-meaning family had placed around her; maybe even take a risk or two. The gilded cage they'd constructed around her had become more and more restricting, making its presence felt more than ever when her consultant had told her she was in remission.

Suddenly, she'd had the green light to live the life she'd dreamt about. But she'd been so fiercely guarded that the longed-for freedom to live had felt too new, too unfamiliar and way too daunting. She'd missed out on the years in which self-confidence and independence should have been built and it had left her desperate to make her dreams come true but unable to believe she had it in her to do so. Her parents hadn't wanted her to become a nurse, but her need to give something back had given her the strength to push through their objections and her own insecurities about her abilities and do her training.

When she'd been offered the job in London a few months ago, her parents had begged her not to leave home, and she'd had to battle with them as well as her own fears about leaving her small home counties town to go and live in the city. But it had been a step towards the bigger goal—if she could move to London and be okay, maybe she could make Australia happen too. Small steps towards the big dream. Eventually, her family had finally understood and given her their blessing. Telling them about Australia had been a whole different story…

Dexter walked back into the cubicle, followed by a patient who most definitely had the 'appendicitis walk'. The young man was bending forward and clutching his right lower-abdomen.

38   WEDDING FLING TO FOREVER

'Hello,' she said, taking the man's arm and guiding him towards the couch. 'I'm Tilly, one of the nurses. What's your name?'

'Sam,' he replied, grimacing.

'Okay, Sam, let's get you on the couch so the doctor can have a look at you. Keep holding your side and I'll swing your legs up.'

Dexter went to wash his hands at the sink. He was the opposite of fun-seeking, immature, unreliable Lachlan, but Dexter Stevens wasn't the sort of man who would tick the boxes that Lachlan had inadvertently taught her she needed ticking. He wasn't fun-seeking, responsibility-shirking Lachlan, but he also wasn't the warm-hearted, considerate, emotionally open, solid man she needed either. He was something entirely different.

She glanced at him as she placed a pillow under Sam's head. Dexter Stevens was an adventure waiting to happen. The pull of him was powerful. If she was honest with herself, it wasn't just the fact that she admired him as a clinician; it wasn't just that he was the very definition of achingly handsome... No, the reason he made her heart bang against her ribs and her breathing deepen was because there was something darkly exciting about him—something forbidden, something risky.

She'd battled her illness and fears. She was over responsibility-shirking Lachlan. And now, despite her head screaming at her to play safe, she really wanted to take a risk.

COLETTE COOPER

* * *

'Any chance of some painkillers?' groaned Sam as Tilly lowered the back of the couch down to allow Dexter to examine him.

'I need to examine you first,' said Dexter. 'How long have you had the pain?' He placed his hands on the obviously tense abdomen.

'Just this morning. It's got worse.' He winced. 'Ow!'

'Relax,' said Dexter, frowning in concentration as his hands methodically palpated, moving towards the right iliac fossa where the pain appeared to be centred.

'I can't; I'm in agony.'

'We'll give you something for the pain in a moment,' said Tilly, smiling down at him.

'Can't you give me something before there's any more prodding?'

'Palpating,' said Dexter. Why did patients insist on using that word? It made the skilled process of assessing abdominal pain sound so crude.

'Pal…what?' replied Sam.

'The technical word for "prodding" is "palpating",' explained Tilly, smiling and giving Sam's arm a light squeeze. 'Some doctors like to be a bit technical; they think it makes them sound clever. Nearly done, though…hang on a moment longer.'

Dexter caught her look as he glanced at her—her eyes sparkling with mischief and her lips not quite suppressing a grin. He got it. It wasn't the first time she'd teased him like that. She'd called him 'a stick-

40 WEDDING FLING TO FOREVER

ler' on her first day in the department, 'a nit-picker' on the third and she'd given a variety of other names to describe what she clearly thought best suited what he saw as his vigilant, perhaps slightly perfectionist, personality at various times since. He was no longer taken aback at what she clearly saw as amusing leg-pulling, and he refused to rise to the bait as she evidently desperately wanted him to. But it was getting increasingly difficult not to respond to the infectious sparkle in her eyes, and he'd had to turn away from her more than once to hide a smile that threatened his own lips.

'Let me know if this hurts,' said Dexter. He pressed onto the abdomen directly above where the appendix lay then released his hand from the area.

'Argh!'

Rebound tenderness—appendicitis. He'd been correct.

'Ten milligrams of morphine titrated to response,' he said, glancing at Tilly. 'I'll get a line in and bleep the surgeons.'

'Surgeons?' said Sam, looking startled.

'You have appendicitis,' replied Dexter, rewashing his hands and reaching for a cannula. 'You'll need an operation to remove the appendix.'

'Won't that morphine take the pain away?'

'It will,' said Dexter, pulling a tourniquet around Sam's arm firmly, 'But not for long, and it won't cure the underlying problem. Sharp scratch…'

'Would you like me to give the explanation about appendicitis?' said Tilly. 'Or would you prefer to?'

He glanced up at her and had the distinct feeling that she wanted *him* to explain. Fine—he could do that.

'Appendicitis is the most common cause of an acute abdomen, and is initiated usually by the obstruction of the lumen of the intestine, leading to inflammation and possibly peritonitis—'

'Perhaps in English?' interrupted Tilly.

He looked up at her again and frowned.

Tilly turned to Sam. 'Sometimes doctors have their own language and forget that everyone else speaks plain English.'

Sam managed a grimacing grin.

'The appendix is a tiny part of the bowel, just here.' She indicated to her own right lower-abdomen. 'It can become inflamed just like anything else can—your tonsils, for example—and once it's inflamed it has to be removed. It's a very simple procedure these days, though. It can be done with keyhole surgery so it won't spoil your six-pack.' She smiled at him and then at Dexter. 'I'll nip out and get your painkiller. Back in a tick. You're doing really well.'

Dexter didn't look up but he could hear her humming to herself as she made her way to the clinical room. Tilly Clover was an excellent nurse but this was another of those times when he had to clench his teeth. She could drive a sane person crazy. What was with the 'doctors have their own language' comment? His explanation, as far as it had gone before she'd interrupted him, was textbook. He could have been a lot more technical if he'd wanted to.

42 WEDDING FLING TO FOREVER

Sliding a cannula into place in Sam's arm, he drew off a set of bloods. And, if she hummed that particular song once more today, he was going to have to tell her to pipe down, or at least hum something different.

'Here we go,' said Tilly, coming back in. 'How are you doing Sam?'

'I'm in agony,' Sam replied, lying on his side, his legs now curled up.

'You'll feel better very quickly when this goes in,' said Tilly.

'Knock, knock.' The cubicle curtain moved slightly.

'Come in,' said Tilly.

'I hear you've got a customer for me?' It was Robert Luscombe. Dexter handed over.

'Twenty-four-year-old, usually fit and well. RIF pain since this morning, steadily getting worse. Tender, guarding, rebound tenderness. Pyrexial at thirty-eight; tachy at one ten. FBC, U&Es and clotting done. Morphine going in as we speak.'

'Any chance of that in English?' said Sam, his face now less contorted with pain.

'Doctor speak again,' said Tilly, rolling her eyes at Sam. 'What he means is that you have all the signs and symptoms of appendicitis, that he's taken a blood sample for tests and that we're giving you some painkiller.' She lowered her voice conspiratorially but kept it just loud enough that Dexter could still hear. 'I should start charging for interpreter services.'

Dexter looked at her and blinked. He'd handed the patient over concisely, providing all the information the surgical reg needed. There was nothing wrong with that, was there?

'Well, it certainly sounds as though you have appendicitis,' said Robert, smiling. 'How's your pain now?'

'Getting better,' said Sam, beginning to relax as Tilly slowly continued to administer the morphine, watching carefully for his response.

'It's good stuff,' said Tilly, removing the syringe and holding it up for Dexter to see. 'Seven mils.'

He nodded. 'Noted.'

'We'll get you up to the ward, Sam,' said Robert, 'and get your operation done this afternoon, so nothing to eat or drink from now; sorry about that.'

Sam nodded, now much more relaxed.

'Have you got any questions?' asked the surgeon.

'How long will I need to stay in hospital?'

'Probably only overnight,' he replied, smiling. 'We don't want you getting too used to the luxurious hospitality here.'

Tilly nudged Sam with her elbow. 'So don't worry about having to learn the language.'

'I'll see you up on the ward, Sam,' said Robert, raising his hand and beaming as he left. 'We'll look after you, don't worry.'

Sam nodded, managing a smile before he closed his eyes.

'Robert's lovely, isn't he?' whispered Tilly, looking at a lightly sleeping Sam.

Dexter had never considered whether Robert Luscombe was lovely or not and wasn't sure how to answer her question. The surgeon had turned up, confirmed the diagnosis and agreed to take the patient to Theatre—that was all he could ask for. Whether he was lovely or not wasn't relevant.

'He's so pleasant and cheerful and friendly,' she continued, her head to one side, as though thinking hard. 'And warm and sociable and…' She brought a finger to her lips and glanced at him, her eyes sparkling with humour. Ah; she was making a point.

'And I'm not?'

Damn it, he'd taken the bait.

She straightened up, pretending to look shocked. 'Oh, I didn't say that,' she protested.

But that was exactly what she'd been saying—and she was right.

She held out her hand towards him. 'If you pass me those bloods, I'll get them sent off.'

'So you're going to the wedding of the year, then?' said Dexter, handing her the bag. The revelation she was going to the wedding without a plus one had been oddly pleasing. Odd, because it didn't make sense—on any level.

'Of course,' she replied. 'A two day south-Indian wedding, held in a castle on the Northumbrian coast, who wouldn't jump at the chance of that?' She tucked a stray wisp of amethyst-highlighted hair behind her ear and cocked her head to one side, as though thinking again. 'Except you, by the sounds of it.'

He shifted his stance uncomfortably. He'd put off replying to the invitation from the CEO and knew exactly why. He hated parties, and he hated wedding-related ones even more. Being a page boy at his auntie's wedding when his father had ruined the reception by slowly getting more and more drunk, increasingly raucous and progressively louder was the first time he'd felt such shame. He'd gone outside after his father had knocked the top tier of the wedding cake to the floor and his auntie's new husband had found him in his hiding place in the branches of a tree.

'I forgot.'

Tilly snorted. 'Forgot? You don't forget anything—you have a brain like a computer.'

'Human brains are far more complex than computers.' He tapped his notes onto his tablet.

'Even more reason not to forget,' said Tilly. 'Well, I'm glad you're going. You don't want to end up with a reputation as being antisocial.'

He glanced up from his tablet, his eyes narrowed. *Was she baiting him again?* He knew his reputation. He kept himself to himself and didn't engage in idle chatter about people's home or personal lives outside of work. People thought he was cool and standoffish. But that was how he liked it. Keeping people at arm's length was far more sensible than opening his arms wide and drawing people in towards him, as Tilly did. To do that would leave him vulnerable, an open target at which others could hurl whatever they felt like hurling. Best to keep a dis-

46 WEDDING FLING TO FOREVER

tance, not get involved and stay below the parapet. He was no Robert Luscombe, and he didn't walk into a room and light it up like Tilly, either.

'Right, I'll get these sent off and arrange for Sleepy Head to go up to the ward,' said Tilly.

'That would be helpful.'

'That's me,' she replied brightly. 'Always helpful. And talking of helpful…' She lowered her voice, even though Sam was now snoring gently. 'I think it would be really helpful to patients if your explanations could be a little less…medical.'

He frowned.

'You think I should give patients less medical explanations of their medical conditions?'

She nodded. 'Ones that are easier to understand.'

'Everyone knows what appendicitis is and anyway there was nothing wrong—'

'Sam didn't seem to,' she interrupted, staring at him, her hands on her hips.

'Wrong with…' he continued, ignoring the challenge in her stunning eyes, 'My explanation—as far as you allowed me to get with it.'

'Just try toning it down a little,' she suggested. 'You could try cracking a smile sometimes, too… like the lovely Robert Luscombe.'

He scowled. 'I'm here to provide medical care to patients, not to be an advert for teeth whitening.'

'I think it's good to make them feel welcome and to provide a friendly face.'

'Patients come to A&E because they need urgent, expert medical care.' He darted a glance at Sam,

COLETTE COOPER 47

who was still sleeping. 'Are you telling me I don't provide that?'

Tilly straightened up, tilting her chin defiantly. 'Not for one second am I doubting that. But you could do all that with a smile occasionally, that's all I'm saying. Try it; it really doesn't hurt.' She jiggled the bag of blood samples. 'I'd better get these sent off.'

She spun on her heel, pulled back the curtain and left the cubicle. In a second, the humming began once again and he drew in a breath. How did she do it? How did she manage to make him want to gaze into her stunning eyes one minute and need to leave the room the next? How could he be so drawn towards her infectious sparkle and undeniable warmth yet find her deeply maddening at the same time?

And exactly why had he felt suddenly compelled to accept Geetha's wedding invitation when he usually avoided parties as a Grinch avoids Christmas?

Because Tilly was going...without a plus one.

And an enticing but puzzling thought had slipped, uninvited into his mind. The wedding was an opportunity to see Tilly somewhere other than work. But he wasn't interested in people's lives outside of work. And, as beautifully hypnotic as her eyes were, and as much as her ever-present sparkle somehow had him on a reel being inexorably drawn towards her, there was no way he wanted anything other than an entirely professional relationship with her.

So why had his heart lifted when she'd said there was no plus one? He drew in a deep breath, letting

48 WEDDING FLING TO FOREVER

it out slowly, controlling it and regaining the power over his errant thoughts.

He wouldn't go to the wedding. But, damn it, he'd told Geetha he would. He ran his fingers through his hair. He'd held off replying to her invitation for weeks, hoping she'd forget she'd invited him, and on a whim he'd stupidly told her he was going.

And Tilly Clover, with her sunshine smile, irrepressible sense of fun and deeply annoying habit of getting under his skin, was the reason.

CHAPTER THREE

RESTING HER HEAD back on the soft towel she'd placed on the lip of the deep bath, Tilly closed her eyes, allowing the warmth of the water to seep into her muscles and inhaling the sweet scent of the jasmine bubbles she'd poured generously into the tub. The suite had a huge bed, a small sitting area with a sofa, a gorgeous view out over the rugged Northumbrian coastline and a large *en suite,* which she'd decided to make the most of before the Mehndi party that evening.

Dexter had clearly not been keen on coming to the wedding, but understanding why was confounding. The CEO had invited all heads of department. Yes, there was a little bit of pressure to attend, but Geetha was an excellent manager and completely lovely; besides which, this was going to be a spectacular event. It had been the talk of the hospital for months.

If Dexter did turn up, he'd probably skulk about in his usual dark, unsmiling manner wishing he were back at work, whereas she fully intended to enjoy the experience to the full and couldn't wait to share Geetha's joy and have a two-day party, whether he came or not. So why was she thinking about him?

Because she wanted him to come. And that thought hit her smack in the centre of her chest.

'You appear to be in the wrong room.'

Tilly's eyes flew open and she sat up, sending a wave of water slopping back and forth violently as she drew in a sharp breath.

'Dexter!' Glad of the thick layer of jasmine bubbles, which came up to her neck, she nevertheless instinctively drew her knees in towards her, hugging them to her chest. Deep blue eyes bored into her, his expression unreadable—calm, assured and impassive, as usual giving nothing away, as though standing there while she was naked in the bath before him was the most natural thing in the world. 'What the hell are you doing here?' She glanced at the shocking pink bra and knickers she'd left strewn on the floor inches from his feet and willed him not to notice them.

'I could ask you the same question.'

'This is *my* room.'

'This is room five.'

'Is it?' She couldn't think straight. If questioned right there and then, she wasn't sure she'd be able to remember her own name.

'You'll have to relocate.' His eyes didn't leave hers for the longest moment but she couldn't read them. Dexter Stevens was master of mask-wearing. *How could he just stand there, impassive, with her shocking pink underwear at his feet and her naked in the bath?*

But his lips parted just slightly, and for a second his gaze strayed from her eyes to her mouth, and he drew in a breath. Perhaps he couldn't mask everything he felt. Emboldened, she lifted her chin. It was he who'd walked in on her, after all. She shouldn't be the one who was embarrassed in all this.

'Do you think you could perhaps wait in the bedroom while I get out of the bath and we can sort this out?'

'I'll unpack while you do that.' He lowered his head as he turned to leave and hesitated a moment, the toe of one of his expensive-looking shoes brushing her abandoned bright pink knickers. She cringed.

'Hang on a second,' she replied, having realised what he'd said. 'Unpack?'

'Take my things out of my bag,' he said, lifting his gaze and walking away.

'What if *you're* in the wrong room?'

He turned and stood in the doorway, his eyes sweeping the room and alighting on her—dark blue, powerful eyes making her pulse quicken and her breathing deepen.

'Well, although you seem to have made yourself very much at home, I was assured that my room was number five—the suite with the family crest of the Tynedales on the door.'

'That's what they told me.'

'Well, there must have been a mistake.'

'You don't say.'

'I'll go back down and tell them to sort it out.'

'You do that.' She watched him leave, waiting for the door to close before exhaling deeply, briefly closing her eyes and trying to slow her heart rate. But, when she opened her eyes, the shocking pink underwear was the first thing she saw, disturbed slightly where Dexter's shoe had inadvertently shifted it.

He'd carefully masked his expression but she knew him well enough to know that the way he'd looked at her was far different from how he'd ever looked at her before. He hadn't quite been able to hide the flame in his deep blue eyes when his gaze had lingered on her lips. The fire that had shot through her had been caused because she'd recognised something in them that hadn't matched the coolness of the words he spoke.

Perhaps spending time with him at the wedding wasn't something she should have looked forward to. She wanted to resist the pull of him, didn't she? He didn't tick the boxes—not even close. There were plenty of people to get to know at this wedding and Dexter Stevens wasn't one of them.

She relaxed back onto the towel, resting her arms on the sides of the roll-topped bathtub and looking around the steamy, luxuriously appointed room with its gold taps, beautiful tiling and large, ornate, gilt-edged mirror that stood propped against the wall in the corner.

She inhaled deeply. She hadn't had a break from work in far too long and she was going to enjoy these few days away. Much as she loved her job at the hospital, doing all the extra shifts was probably more than her consultant would advise. Her leukaemia had been in remission for eight years but Dr Banerjee, her lovely haematologist whom she now only had to see once a year, would likely have told her to slow down just a little. Moving out to Australia wasn't going to come cheaply, though, and seeing the money from the extra shifts building up in her account each month only spurred her on to do more.

Besides, the department was rarely fully staffed and shifts needed to be filled. As one of the senior nurses in A&E, the responsibility to ensure patient safety fell to her and she was *never* going to compromise that.

The water had cooled. Picking up her phone from the stand by the bath, she glanced at the time. There was an hour before the Mehndi party. Leaning forward, she opened the hot tap. Ten more minutes to relax would be fine. Closing her eyes and leaning back, the water quickly warming again, her thoughts wandered back to Dexter.

What if there hadn't been an error with the room? What if they had come here together, as a couple, for the long weekend in this beautiful castle *intentionally…*?

A delicious warmth spread through her and it wasn't solely due to the hot water running from the tap. She let her imagination fly… They'd spend most of the weekend in that huge bed in the next room, having food delivered when they wanted it, leaving the *do not disturb* sign on the door in between times, perhaps sharing this bath, soaping each other's bodies…

'You're going to flood the bathroom!'

She gasped and her eyes flew open to see Dexter

striding across the room towards her looking hor-
rified, reaching for the tap, turning it off, reaching
down into the water yanking out the plug.

'What have you done that for?' Her heart thumped
against her ribs at his sudden, unexpected and violent arrival.

'You were about to flood the place.' The sleeve
of his shirt was dripping and covered in bath foam
and he shook his arm, flinging foam in all directions. 'Had you fallen asleep?'

'No,' she replied indignantly, frowning and once
more crossing her arms over her chest.

*Had she? Had she, once again, been dreaming
about him?*

'I was just relaxed.'

'Too relaxed; I'm soaked.' He began to unbutton
his shirt and her heart rate climbed further, but not
with shock this time. Pulling the shirt from his back,
he took hold of the sleeve and squeezed it over the
water, then shook it out, turned and draped it over
a towel rail. A perfect six-pack was revealed all too
briefly before he turned, but she now had a view of
his broad back—the powerful, wide shoulders ta-
pering to his waist and carved muscles that moved
beautifully beneath smooth, bronzed skin.

He turned to face her, hands curving over the
waistband of his dark jeans. Her breathing deepened
and she swallowed, wanting but unable to look away.

He was perfect.

She was naked.

She was right. There *had been* a heavenly body hiding away beneath those navy scrubs.

'It turns out there has been a mistake with the room after all,' he said.

Somehow, she found her voice. 'Oh, well, I hope they've put you in a room as nice as this one. Thanks for letting me know.'

'It's not quite as straightforward as that.'

Her heart sank. They'd put *her* in the wrong room. And he was clearly expecting her to be the one to move. 'I've hung all my things up now. You haven't unpacked yet. Couldn't *you* have the other room?'

'There is no other room.'

She shivered just as the bath let out a gurgle as the last of the water drained away, leaving her naked apart from the abundance of bubbles that still covered her.

'Do you think you could perhaps turn around if you're staying to debate this further?' She held up her arm, swirling her hand to indicate to him to look the other way. 'What do you mean, no other room?'

'They're fully booked,' he replied, reaching for a white towel from a neatly folded pile on a dressing table and passing it to her. 'Here.'

She took the towel from him, wrapping it around herself but remaining seated in the bath. He stepped back and turned round, his hands on his hips. Her gaze travelled the length of him, from his dark head to broad shoulders. Angular muscles slid over each other as he adjusted his stance, putting more weight

56 WEDDING FLING TO FOREVER

on one leg, his hips tilting, drawing her gaze to his firm ass and down his long legs.

She closed her eyes briefly. 'Have they suggested another hotel?'

'We're in a tiny village that's hosting a huge wedding. Every room is booked. The nearest hotel with a vacancy is sixty miles away, back in town.'

'You're kidding me.'

'Does it look as though I'm kidding you?'

It looked as though he'd walked straight out of the pages of a celebrity special feature in a high-end glossy magazine. And he wasn't the sort of man who would 'kid'.

'So what have they suggested?' She pulled the towel tighter.

'I didn't hang around to find out. They've messed up and there's not much anyone can do about it.'

'This is because you didn't RSVP to Geetha on time.' This was his fault.

'The fact that the hotel has double-booked this room has nothing to do with the very slight delay in my RSVP and everything to do with their incompetence. I'll just go home. I didn't want to come anyway.'

'No, no, no, you're not getting away that easily. Is there honestly no other room?'

Dexter spun round. 'Why would I lie about it?'

Tilly swirled her hand at him again and he turned back round. 'Because it would be a perfect excuse not to stay for the wedding. You clearly didn't want to come, for some weird reason, and this would be

COLETTE COOPER

a good get-out. Well, you have to stay, you're committed now.'

'And where am I supposed to sleep—in the dungeon?'

'It might be the best place for you if you're going to be so grumpy. No, you can sleep here. It's a huge room and it's only for two nights.'

He turned round again, his eyes wide.

'And where are you going to sleep?'

'Will you stop turning back around? I'm naked beneath these bubbles, thank you very much.'

He carefully held her gaze, as though if he let his concentration slip even for a second it would travel down her body. 'Sorry.' He closed his eyes and turned away.

'In answer to your question,' she continued, 'I'll sleep here too. It's a double room, after all.'

'There's only one bed.'

'Sherlock Holmes had better watch out.'

'Very funny.'

'Well, we just have to make the best of it, don't we? You've told Geetha you'll be here, and she'll be hurt if you're not.'

'I'm sure she'd understand.'

'She won't because we're not telling her. This is her wedding weekend and I'm not having her stressed because of some silly room booking error. She need never know.'

'And what about everyone else? The other people here—other staff from the hospital?'

'They don't need to know either.'

58   WEDDING FLING TO FOREVER

Her phone alarm went off, making her jump. She silenced it.

'I need to get ready for the Mehndi party. So, are we agreed?'

She watched his torso expand as he drew in a breath. 'I suppose there's no option, is there?'

'No. You go and unpack and get changed, then, while I dry off. We've got exactly twenty minutes to get ready.'

He walked out of the bathroom.

'Close the door on the way out,' she called after him.

He reached behind him without turning round, grabbed the door and pulled it closed.

They were going to have to share this room. For the next two nights.

She climbed out of the bath and stood on the rug, clutching the towel around her. She shivered. But whether the shiver was due to her body temperature dropping from getting out of the warmth of the bath, or from the thought of spending the next two nights in a fairy-tale castle with Dexter Stevens, owner of that flawless torso, she wasn't at all sure.

CHAPTER FOUR

DEXTER BRACED HIS hands on the stone windowsill and screwed his eyes shut, before opening them again and staring out onto the courtyard below without seeing the view at all.

Why hadn't he knocked before barging in?

He'd been so annoyed with the room booking fiasco—and himself for causing it—that propriety had eluded him completely. And suddenly he'd been standing in the bathroom with Tilly's dignity being shielded only by bath bubbles. Once he'd dealt with the threat of the bathroom being flooded, his horror at having walked in on her had all but paralysed him. He'd dealt with it the only way he knew how—by ignoring the way his heart had thudded in his chest and discounting the searing heat that had flooded his veins. He'd done what he always did—carefully masked his expression and turned his back on feeling anything.

Feelings were dangerous—they got a person hurt. How many times had he trusted the side of his father that had given him hope that things might change? How often had he longed for more of those brief moments when his father had been sober, smiled at him, told him a silly joke or taken him to the corner shop to buy him a bag of sweets? Those moments had never lasted long but he'd still cherished them. He'd always waited for the next time, always believed that one day his father would stop drinking and be like the other dads.

But that had never happened. His father had never changed. And eventually Dexter had given up hoping. Trying to love someone who didn't love him back...enduring disappointment after disappointment, one rejection after another...was exhausting. It hurt. Having feelings for someone made a person vulnerable to all those things. It had made him vulnerable when Helena, the only woman he'd ever lost his heart to, had thrown his love for her back in his face. He *had* loved her despite the fact that, according to her, her reason for cheating on him was that he hadn't. But he had loved her; hell, he'd even wondered if they might have a future together.

He hadn't been enough for her, though, had he? And she'd been very clear about why that was—she'd wanted someone who would make her feel loved and cherished. Obviously, taking her to great restaurants, splashing out on luxurious holidays and buying her just about anything she wanted hadn't hit the mark. As it had turned out, she'd wanted the whole hearts and flowers, mushy, sentimental nonsense that he had no idea how to deliver. She'd wanted to get inside his head, have long talks about his past and about feelings. He wasn't that sort of man.

And he didn't want to feel any more. He'd rather be numb. Numbness had a beautiful, safe simplicity, and emotions ruined it.

His father's final rejection of him, some four years

ago when he'd been in the last stages of liver failure on the palliative care ward, had come the same week as Helena's scathing appraisal of his shortcomings. He'd known his father's days were numbered. The liver cirrhosis had been in its final stages and Dexter had thought that his father might be a little more forgiving, given that he was coming to the end of his life.

His father had always enjoyed reading the sports pages in the newspaper, so he'd taken a paper to read to him on the ward—his father had been too weak by then to read it himself. But, instead of his father being pleased he'd tried to do something thoughtful, he'd snarled, scornfully telling him if he hadn't brought him a hip flask of whisky he might as well go home.

So Dexter had left, hoping to find some understanding from Helena. But he'd opened the front door to her house and seen a man hurriedly leaving by the back door, with Helena standing there in a bathrobe.

Which was exactly why he was never going to feel anything for anyone ever again. He was never going to be at the mercy of anyone else. Rejection hurt and took way too long to get over. His father was gone and Dexter had been released from continually trying and failing to be accepted by him. Helena was ancient history. The only women he occasionally hooked up with now always knew the score. He only did short term—very short term—and it was only ever physical. No one would ever get into his head

62 WEDDING FLING TO FOREVER

again, including Tilly, despite her oddly captivating vivacity and enchanting eyes, and whether they had to share a room together or not.

He sighed heavily, still staring into space. He was still annoyed with himself. Tilly had been right— this was his fault. He'd delayed replying to the CEO's invitation because, stupidly, he'd hoped that by some miracle Geetha might not have noticed he'd not replied and he could get away with not going.

He hated parties. He loathed weddings. And this was an intolerable two-day mix of them both.

Turning away from the window, he caught his reflection in the long mirror that stood beside the wardrobe. Opening his suitcase, he drew out the shirt he'd brought to wear that evening, slipping it on. He didn't need a psychologist to work out why he felt the way he did about events like this and why he was much more comfortable being in the controlled, well-ordered world of A&E, where policies, protocols and procedures drove what people did and how they reacted to situations. Parties required easy conversation skills, the ability to schmooze, the obligatory consumption of large amounts of alcohol, singing and dancing...

He closed his eyes. He'd seen enough raucous parties to last him a lifetime. He didn't know whether his father had always been dependent on alcohol or if his drinking had only started after his mother had died giving birth to Dexter. What he did know was that he'd rarely seen his father sober. Although he'd drink when he was alone, he'd often go to the pub, bringing a few mates back home afterwards. Trying to go to sleep with a thin pillow wrapped around his head to block out the noise and then going to school the next day so tired he could barely keep his eyes open had been commonplace for Dexter.

So, no, he didn't need a psychologist to tell him that he hated parties because they reminded him of a childhood dominated by his father's drinking and terrifying volcanic rages, in which he'd never had the presence of a mum who might have cared he existed.

'Would you mind just fastening this necklace for me, please?'

He turned round. Tilly stood just outside the bathroom door in an ankle-length, softly flowing dress of rich, peacock colours, holding a gold chain around her neck ready to be fastened. He'd never seen her in anything other than her blue uniform scrubs and the difference was startling. Her glossy, dark hair was loose around her shoulders, the subtle amethyst highlights catching the light, matching her exquisite eyes. She was beautiful.

Standing behind her and moving her hair to one side, he took the ends of the chain from her fingers, their warmth infusing his own. He moved her hair back into place, his fingers lingering a moment longer than they needed to, savouring the softness of her hair and inhaling the light, floral scent of her.

'Thank you.' Her sing-song voice had returned, in contrast to the unfamiliar accusatory tone she'd

64   WEDDING FLING TO FOREVER

used earlier. 'Are you ready to go down? Love the shirt…very vibrant.'

He looked down at the shirt he'd bought to comply with the dress code of 'bright colours'.

'I guess,' he replied. *Let's get this thing over with.*

'Ever been to one of these before?' asked Tilly, slipping on her sandals and picking up her bag.

'No.' He picked up the room key and slipped it into his pocket. 'Have you?'

'No. I've asked around about them, though. Traditionally the Mehndi party was for women only—a bit like a hen party—but more commonly these days men attend them too, so it's more of a pre-wedding party. You obviously read the memo about brightly coloured clothes.'

'I did.'

'I'm looking forward to getting some henna.'

'Henna?'

'Having your henna done is mandatory at a Mehndi. It's all about the bride having hers done, really, but all the guests have at least a little tattoo.'

'Seriously?'

'Oh, yes.' Tilly looked at him earnestly…almost too earnestly. He narrowed his eyes, unsure whether to believe her. He was getting used to her mischievous teasing.

'It's mandatory?'

'Absolutely. Come on.' She pulled open the door.

Great. They descended the spiral stone staircase in single file, Dexter squeezing and stretching his fists as they walked. The guests at this wedding weren't going to be the drunken, out-of-control losers his father had brought to their home.

Relax, Stevens. None of them are your father, either. There couldn't be many people on this earth—if any—who could match *his* violent temper.

He swallowed. Except maybe himself. The fear he'd lived with all his life crept from the dark recesses in his brain where he tried so hard to keep it buried. A demon that lurked so deeply but, no matter how hard he tried to not acknowledge it, refused to be ignored or silenced.

What if he was like his father? What if, under the right circumstances—after a drink or in difficult emotional situations—he too had the propensity to be engulfed in the red mist, to let it cloud his judgement so he became enraged, violent and dangerous?

He'd inherited his father's temper—that had been made clear very early on in his life.

He'd lashed out at Harvey Larkin at school that time when he'd been ribbed about his uniform being too small and his trainers being a supermarket brand. The red mist had clouded his judgement then, just for a moment, and he'd struck the boy. He'd been given detention and his father had beaten him when he'd arrived home late.

'If—you're—going to—beat someone—up,' he'd shouted in between striking Dexter with the leather belt he kept by his chair in the living room, 'do it where—no one—can—see you.'

He didn't want to have inherited that vile, destructive temper—he didn't want to repeat the cycle. But he was his father's son; he'd grown up surrounded by violence, so it must still be within him to be unable to control it, but Dexter would let hell freeze over before allowing that to happen. The only way to ensure that it didn't happen was to control every emotion before it controlled him.

They exited the dimly lit stairwell out into the early evening summer sunshine of the grassy courtyard. A white marquee decked with bunting stood in the centre and a huge archway of brilliantly coloured flowers surrounded its entrance. There were food stations dotted around and tables and chairs set out, again bedecked with flowers. People were mingling, chatting, smiling and laughing, and they were all dressed in clothes far brighter than his own. Tilly took two glasses of champagne from a tray offered by a waiter and handed one to him.

He took the glass—it was expected—but he wasn't going to drink it. He'd only ever touched alcohol once, aged fifteen. His father's so-called friends had been around and they'd offered him a can of beer—more than offered, really, as they'd jeered him when he'd refused at first. And then it had occurred to him: if he joined them, his father might like him as much as he liked them. He never shouted at his drinking buddies; he never lashed out at them. Maybe he could become like them—have more of his father's better side, earn the respect he showed for his friends and be accepted. So he'd had the can...and then another...and then a proffered whisky.

He remembered throwing up. He remembered them laughing. He remembered vowing never to be in that position again. But he never stopped wanting his father's approval; never stopped trying to earn his acceptance.

That was what feelings did to people.

'Look at all this—it's fabulous,' said Tilly, turning to him, a thrilled, excited, beautiful smile lighting her face with joy that somehow, inexplicably, made him want to smile back. She tugged at his arm, leading the way. 'Come on; I can see Geetha over there.'

'Dexter, Tilly…so glad you made it. Come and meet Vijesh.' Geetha indicated towards a tall, distinguished looking man wearing a traditional South Indian kurta tunic of royal blue with batik patterns and bronze-coloured trousers. 'Are your rooms okay?'

Dexter opened his mouth to speak as they followed her across the grass towards the groom.

'Gorgeous,' replied Tilly, shooting him a look that told him in no uncertain terms to shut up. 'So, what's the order of events for this evening?'

'Oh, it's very relaxed,' Geetha replied. 'No formalities this evening; it's just a big pre-wedding party. Lots of food and dancing. Are you going to have some henna?'

'Absolutely. Dexter's going to have one too.'

'Excellent,' said Geetha. 'This is Vijesh. Vijesh, this is Tilly, a sister in A&E; and this is Dexter, lead consultant.'

'Pleased to meet you,' said Vijesh, shaking each

68 WEDDING FLING TO FOREVER

of their hands. 'Thank you for coming. Can I get you a drink?'

And so it began. Tilly followed the very friendly and clearly very happy groom to one of the drinks stations, where she chose the fruit punch, which came with a ridiculously large paper umbrella and pink plastic straw. Dexter asked for orange juice, removing the accompanying straw and umbrella, leaving them on the bar. Tilly lifted her glass, chinking it against the one Vijesh held, and then against his.

'Happy Mehndi!'

Vijesh smiled then turned as Geetha called his name, summoning him to go and mingle with some other guests.

'You should have had the umbrella,' said Tilly as they made their way over to check out the various food stations dotted about the courtyard. 'It would have completed your outfit.'

'At least I feel slightly less overdressed, now I'm here,' he replied. 'But this...' he tugged at his shirt '...is going to the charity shop as soon as I get home.'

'Don't be such a sour puss.' She plucked the pink straw from her glass and plonked it into his orange juice with a grin. 'Here...lean into the vibe, not away from it. Let's get some food.'

He didn't want to lean into the vibe. He hated parties and didn't believe in happy-ever-afters. The only reason he was here at all was because of a professional obligation.

But that wasn't entirely accurate, was it? He was here because Tilly was here...without a plus one.

Because the thought of spending time with her had been too tempting to turn down. He'd wanted to see more of that light that shone from her eyes and came from deep within her soul, the intrinsic joy which radiated from her and the almost infectious ability to delight in just about everything. Where did that come from? And why did it compel him to want to be around her?

He ladled some food into a bowl, watching her as she picked up some bread and a spoon and wandered over to the nearest table, at which sat an older couple. He followed her.

'Hello, I'm Tilly and this is Dexter. Do you mind if we join you?'

'Please, sit down,' said the woman, smiling at Tilly.

'Isn't this beautiful?' said Tilly, pulling out a chair and looking around, her face full of wonder. 'It's like a fairy tale.'

The woman smiled. 'It is. I can't believe my granddaughter is getting married in a castle.'

'Geetha is your granddaughter?' asked Tilly.

And the three of them began chatting away, as though they'd known each other all their lives.

How did she do that so easily—just wander up to strangers and start a conversation? *He* could wander up to strangers but only if they were patients in his department. Chatting away to someone randomly, especially about something non-medical, was a very alien concept and not one he ever indulged in. He

70 WEDDING FLING TO FOREVER

knew where his comfort zone lay—and it wasn't in places like this.

Suddenly Geetha's grandfather, sitting opposite, coughed. Dexter looked up sharply. The man coughed again and struggled to draw in a breath. He was choking. Dexter got to his feet, strode round to the other side of the table and slapped him sharply on the back between his shoulder blades, five times. But the elderly man clutched at his throat, staring up at Dexter with wide, terrified eyes.

In a second, Tilly was by his side, speaking to the man who was bending forward, desperately struggling for air.

'You're going to be fine.' Her calm voice was soothing, reassuring. 'Dexter is an A&E consultant and he's going to give you a sharp hug from behind to dislodge what you swallowed.'

The back blows weren't working. The breaths the poor man was trying to take were noisy and rasping. He had to try abdominal thrusts. He was aware that Geetha's grandmother had risen from her seat and that a few of the other guests had done the same and made their way towards the rapidly unfolding scene.

Grasping him firmly from behind, Dexter wrapped his arms around the quickly tiring man, one fist clasping the other just below the xiphisternum, thrusting upwards. He glanced at Tilly but the tiniest shake of her head told him it hadn't worked.

'And again,' said Tilly, addressing the man. 'You're doing really well.'

But the man was beginning to tire. Dexter braced

himself again and gave a second thrust, once more glancing at Tilly, who was on her phone, dialling for an ambulance. But an ambulance wasn't going to get there before it was too late. This was on him. The old man had become a little heavier, taking less of his own weight. He had seconds before the man collapsed completely. More people had made their way towards them to see what was going on. He braced again; thrust once more.

Tilly...?

She shook her head, her eyes meeting his, their sparkle gone, saying more than words ever could.

The man slumped. Dexter took his weight, easing him to the ground and lying him on his back. He wasn't breathing. His airway was completely blocked.

'Grandpa!' Geetha ran towards them but Tilly caught her and held her gently back, giving Dexter room to do what he needed to.

An emergency tracheotomy. On a field, in a castle courtyard. Without any equipment.

He reached up onto the table where he remembered seeing a knife. Extending the old man's neck, he located the thyroid cartilage and, moving his fingers downwards, found the cricoid. Placing the knife, he sliced into the cricothyroid membrane and into the trachea, rotating it to widen the opening he'd made.

He looked up at Tilly. 'Straw.'

Thankfully, she realised what he was doing and grabbed the pink plastic straw discarded from his

72 WEDDING FLING TO FOREVER

drink and handing it to him, still holding onto Geetha's hand. Inserting the straw into the opening he'd made, he blew two breaths into it, watching for the chest expanding as his own breath filled the old man's lungs.

It worked. Dexter watched him, willing him.

Come on, breathe.

A gasp from the old man. A collective release of breath from the gathered crowd.

Instantly, Tilly knelt down on the grass beside them, tugging Geetha down with her, taking the old man's hand.

'Hello, there. Try not to speak. Some food went down the wrong way but you're doing fine now. You're okay. Geetha's here.'

Dexter watched them, his fingers still holding the plastic straw in place as he drew his phone from his pocket and called the emergency services, to change Tilly's request for an ambulance to one for a helicopter. Geetha's grandpa was alive but he wasn't out of the woods yet.

Tilly had her arm around Geetha's shoulders and was reassuring both of them. Geetha's grandma joined them, looking relieved, her hand to her chest. Tilly took her hands in her own and spoke to her, and the old lady smiled back at her, opening her arms to embrace her as a spontaneous round of applause broke out. Dexter finished speaking to ambulance control and slipped his phone back into his pocket, looking up and realising that everyone was looking at him. Tilly was clapping too and beaming at him.

'Thank you, Dexter.' It was Geetha. She opened her arms wide. 'You saved his life.' And suddenly he was in her arms, being squeezed, one hand still holding onto the straw, the other like a rod at his side.

'They're sending an air ambulance,' said Dexter.

Geetha released him but her arms were immediately replaced by those of her grandma, who gave him an enormous squeeze before letting him go. Others came forward to shake his hand and grasp him by a shoulder, thanking him. He didn't need to be thanked for what he'd done. He'd just been doing his job.

'Well done,' said Tilly, giving him a smile that could have launched the proverbial thousand ships but which made him glance away quickly.

Tilly Clover smiled almost all the time…at everyone. But when she directed that smile at him, happiness shining out of her eyes, he found more and more that, beautiful as it was, it challenged him…in ways he didn't want to be challenged. The more he saw of her smile, the more he wanted to make her smile— be the cause of it; look into her amethyst eyes, into her beautiful soul, and stay there. Because somehow he imagined that doing that would make him feel as a ship's crew felt finally docking in a safe harbour after battling though a maelstrom…or like coming in from a snowstorm to a warm fire. It was enticing, inviting and becoming increasingly difficult to ignore.

Tilly Clover was different. He was drawn to her in a way he'd never been drawn to a woman...ever. This was more than physical...much more.

Tilly Clover—with her sometimes annoying in the extreme sing-song voice, captivating, twinkling eyes, tempting smile and irrepressible zest for life was more than a woman he simply wanted to take to bed. He wanted to look at her, listen to her, be with her...absorb her, somehow. Since Helena, he hadn't had a relationship that had lasted longer than a couple of nights and he'd made very sure that any woman he was with knew the score from the outset.

No promises.

No commitment.

No emotion involved.

And no way on earth could he ever be hurt, humiliated or rejected. That was how Dexter Stevens did relationships now. But Tilly presented him with a problem. She tempted him to want more.

But he wasn't that sort of man. Helena had rammed that fact home with relish the night his father had died and she'd been in bed with another man—a man who'd been able to provide everything he apparently couldn't.

She'd been right though, hadn't she? He wasn't capable of being the sort of man who deserved a happy-ever-after. At least he knew his limitations. He wasn't capable of feeling love. That normal, human ability had been beaten out of him a long time ago by a father with two sides. Sober, his father had seemed to care—he'd spend time with his son, joke or laugh, kick a ball about in the garden. But, after a drink, the accusations, sarcasm and anger would build quickly and, eventually, Dexter had learned that it was never safe to try to be close to him. Love wasn't to be trusted—a shadow of fear always hovered underneath it.

'Good job I didn't turn my nose up at the straw, like you did.'

He glanced at her. Her generous lips were pressed together as she attempted to suppress a smile, which was clearly proving impossible, and her eyes sparkled with mischief. His stomach clenched and it took more effort than he could ever have thought possible to drag his gaze away from her.

He had to stop this. He had to put distance between them; stay away from the temptation of her. How that was going to be possible, when for weeks he'd been drawn towards her more and more, was impossible to imagine. But, if he didn't stop thinking about her in the way he had been doing, the danger of wanting her would only grow.

He'd keep his distance. She was just a colleague and would remain so. He could manage that.

And then he remembered the sleeping arrangements...

CHAPTER FIVE

'I MIGHT GO back to the room,' said Dexter, glancing round. The helicopter medics had taken Geetha's grandpa to hospital and everyone had dispersed, resuming the festivities.

'No,' said Tilly. 'There are cocktails to try and dancing to be done yet.'

'Not really my thing,' said Dexter.

'It's *everyone's* thing.'

'Except for me.'

'One cocktail…and a dance.'

'I don't drink.'

Tilly blinked at him, looking surprised.

'And I don't dance.'

'Of course you do.'

'I really don't.'

'But it's a wedding.'

'And I've shown my face—done what's expected of me—and now I'm going to my room.'

'Our room,' she corrected.

'Quite,' he replied, dropping his gaze. He'd afforded himself the luxury of not thinking about the night ahead and every possible ramification that might ensue…until now. 'You get a drink and dance if you want to. I'm leaving.'

'Okay,' she replied, 'you've done pretty well this evening.'

'I was just doing my job,' he replied.

She frowned for a moment and then smiled. 'Not the trachy... I meant turning up. The completely non-Dexter bright shirt...not too shabby for a party pooper. You'll have to do better tomorrow, though, for the wedding.'

His heart sank like a lead weight to the very bottom of his stomach. She was letting him off the hook with the Mehndi party but tomorrow was a whole new day, and a whole new fresh hell of pretending that he was happy to be there.

He made his way back towards the castle. A man, clearly sight-impaired, walked past with a beautiful chocolate Labrador guide dog, making Dexter smile. He loved dogs. They were so much less complicated than humans—they asked for little, loved unconditionally and were devoid of the painful, complex baggage just about every human being carried around with them.

Murphy, his childhood dog, had been his port in the storm that was his father. Coming home from school had been like rolling dice. If his father was in the house and had been drinking all day, it never took much to set him off: a tear in his uniform; muddy shoes; growing too tall for his trousers and asking for new ones... But Murphy had always been there, welcoming him home, treating him as though it didn't matter that he was only Dexter, a frightened schoolboy with grubby shoes and too short trousers. To Murphy, he was superman.

Making his way up the spiral stone staircase, he opened the huge wooden door to the room and kicked off his shoes. He walked over to the mullioned window and looked at the grass courtyard below. The party was in full swing. Flashing coloured lights swirled away beneath the white canvas of the huge marquee, and the distant pulsing of the music could be heard even though the room was three floors up. No doubt Tilly was in there, dancing, having a great time, being the life and soul of the party. He smiled. Well, good for her. She was clearly a work hard, play hard kind of woman—not a *party pooper* like him. No doubt she'd be at least a couple of hours yet. He'd take a shower and crack on with the audit paper he needed to finish.

Minutes later soothing, hot water cascaded over him and he lifted his face, closing his eyes, an image of Tilly in her peacock-coloured dress slipping unwanted into his mind. He hadn't wanted to leave her—leave the party, yes, but not leave Tilly. He snapped open his eyes. He didn't want her popping into his head; he didn't want to wish he was still with her. How had she managed to take up so much of his head space?

It was because, somehow, he'd become fascinated by her. By her ability to be everything to everyone: a technically skilled and knowledgeable practitioner; a strong advocate for her team of staff; an empathic support for patients; someone people immediately warmed to... A strikingly beautiful woman he wanted to spend more time with.

Stop.

She was way out of his league. Tilly would want

someone just like her—someone fun, sociable and outgoing. She needed someone who was as in touch with their feelings as she was; someone who was as warm and demonstrative as herself. Not someone who'd rather pull out his own fingernails than feel emotion. There was nothing about him that would interest someone like Tilly. Anyway, he didn't want to get involved with anyone. Relationships came with expectations, and he fell well short of being able to meet any expectations in that field...obviously.

Turning off the shower, he reached for a towel and wrapped it round his waist before stepping out from behind the screen.

'Touché.'

His eyes flew open. Tilly stood on the threshold between the bathroom and the bedroom beyond, arms folded, leaning against the door frame and grinning.

'Touché?' he managed, wiping water from his eyes.

'As in, you walked in on me and now I've walked in on you. At least you have a towel, though; I only had bubbles.'

Heat rose within him. 'I didn't expect you back this early.'

'Clearly,' said Tilly, looking him up and down. His stomach clenched at having her eyes on him. She was openly appraising him; a perfect, dark eyebrow rose as her eyes swept over him. His breathing deepened. She smiled slowly, a finger coming to her full lips, as though contemplating something. She reached up behind the door, grabbed a white towelling bath robe and tossed it to him. He caught it but the action caused the towel around his waist to slip and fall to the floor. Just in time, he drew the robe closer.

'To hide your blushes…' Her gaze seared his, and for the briefest moment her amethyst eyes darkened, making his stomach tighten. Her fingers played with the necklace at her throat.

He lifted his arm, twirling his hand as she'd done earlier. 'Perhaps you should turn around.'

A smile played at the corners of her lips and she shook her head slowly, her eyes not leaving his. It was the most seductive smile he'd ever seen.

'Not the same situation at all, Dexter. I came to see if I could drag you to the party—the band are excellent.'

'I told you—I don't do dancing.'

'No, you said, but why not? You've come all this way; why not enjoy it?'

'I can't think of anything worse.'

She stood up straight and scowled at him. 'What a grumpy-boots you are, Dexter Stevens. If it's just the dancing you don't like, we could have a drink instead.'

'I told you, I don't drink either.'

'Come with me and just enjoy the atmosphere, then. It's a lovely warm, summer evening and the marquee and the courtyard look amazing with the flowers and the lights.'

'I have work to do.'

'Instead of being at a party?' She stared at him as though he'd just arrived from another planet.

'Much more preferable,' he confirmed. 'And it's getting a little chilly, standing here, so do you mind…?' He nodded towards the bedroom, not keen to let go of the robe he held in front of him.

But it didn't seem to bother Tilly. He drew in a breath, steadying his heart rate. She'd locked eyes with him just then with an assured confidence that was sexy in the extreme.

'I don't mind at all.' She grinned and lifted an eyebrow seductively. She'd never looked at him like that at work. But this wasn't the hospital, was it? They were in a fairy-tale castle on the wild Northumbrian coast, far away from reality.

And it was a wedding. People got all sorts of ideas at weddings. Damn the stupid hotel for getting the room booking wrong and putting him in this position.

He nodded again towards the door. 'You go back down if you want to. Don't let me stop you.'

She pouted, looking forlorn. 'But you are stopping me.'

'I'm really not, Tilly. I've told you to go back to the party a number of times now.'

'But I hate the thought of you sitting up here on your own…working on some stuffy work.'

'I like doing audits.'

She rolled her eyes and sagged dramatically,

82 WEDDING FLING TO FOREVER

hanging her head. 'If you don't come to the party, I'll lose my bet.'

His eyes widened. 'You bet on me going to the party?'

She bit her lip, looking up at him from beneath long, dark lashes. 'Only a little.'

'You're kidding me.'

She grimaced. 'So, you either have to come to the party or at least tell me why you won't.' She lifted her chin, challenging him with her gaze. 'And the reason needs to be way more convincing than you having to do an audit.'

It was as though she could see into his soul; as though she knew that he didn't *need* to do the audit tonight. The audit had been his oven-ready excuse if, despite wanting to try to go to the party and feel comfortable about it, he found that he actually couldn't face it.

'I can't believe you did that.'

'It was only with myself.'

'You bet with yourself?'

'I thought I'd be able to persuade you.'

He shook his head, running his fingers through his wet hair, but felt the robe slip and held onto it again.

'That's ridiculous.'

'The bet or me trying to get you to enjoy yourself?'

'Both.'

'And what's wrong with wanting to have a good time, Dexter?' She moved away from the door frame. 'I just wanted to see if there was a different side to you outside of the hospital. A side that wasn't all seriousness and solemnity…perhaps a side that could relax, have fun, be friendly. I'm sure those things are in there…somewhere. You should let them come out to play once in a while. What's life for if you don't?'

She left, closing the door softly behind her.

He let out a breath. She'd done it again. Just as he'd thought he was still in control, she'd confronted him head-on, threatening to breach the barricades that had kept him safe for so long. Tilly Clover had once again ruffled the very fabric of his carefully constructed and controlled world, stopped him in his tracks and made him think.

He'd agreed to come to this wedding because he liked Geetha and didn't really want to let her down but, more than that, he'd liked the prospect of spending time with Tilly. But he'd known there'd be parties involved, and he'd known he absolutely didn't want to go to them, so what the hell was he doing there? It was because he was fascinated by her… drawn to her. So drawn to her that he was rapidly losing his senses. Tilly Clover was testing him like he'd never been tested.

He rubbed his hair and face roughly with the towel. He had to take back control. He needed to stop thinking about her all the time. She didn't have to affect him in this way…or in any way at all. She was just someone he worked with and, for a couple

84 WEDDING FLING TO FOREVER

of nights, with whom he was being forced to share a room for a work function. That was all.

But the way she'd met his gaze just then, with that all-seeing, sexy-as-hell glimmer in her eyes, had heated his blood it didn't seem cooling down was likely to happen any time soon.

CHAPTER SIX

TILLY GLANCED AT the now closed bathroom door. Maybe he didn't want to be looked at. Maybe she'd looked at him in the wrong way.

As if she wanted him.

Which she did.

She walked over to the window that looked out over the courtyard below. Part of her wished she was still down there, dancing. But another part of her wanted to stay in the room. With Dexter.

He'd been determined not to stay any longer at the Mehndi party but, as he'd turned to walk away, just before he'd dropped his gaze, he'd faltered... It had only been for a second, but she'd caught his look—that of a child who wasn't sure which way to go.

Why didn't he like socialising? Why was he so closed off?

The bathroom door opened and Dexter came out, a towel secured around his waist. Maybe he didn't mind being looked at after all.

'It's too hot for the bathrobe,' he said, by way of explanation.

He'd towel-dried his hair but it was still damp and tousled. A lock of it fell loosely over one eye. He flicked his head to dislodge it but it stubbornly fell back. He was a tall, strong, bronzed tower of masculinity and her fingers wanted to find out what he felt like.

'Bathroom free now?' she asked.

'All yours.'

Closing the bathroom door behind her, Tilly pulled her dress over her head and draped it on a hook on the door. She squeezed toothpaste onto her toothbrush and stared at her reflection in the mirror as she brushed.

Did the towel around his waist mean he hadn't brought nightwear? Were they both going to be naked in that bed together? She rinsed and glanced back into the mirror, her eyes going to the pale scar on the right side of her chest. The portacath had helped to save her life, and having a scar was a small price to pay, but she was conscious of it nevertheless. Her fingers went to it. The scar had lightened a little in the years since they'd last pumped the chemo into it, but it was still a reminder of a difficult time—lost years, years to be made up.

She put on the too-big bath robe, pulling the tie at the waist and taking a deep breath before opening the door to the bedroom. Was tonight going to be one of those times when lost years could be made up for?

Dexter was at the desk typing, his laptop open. He'd pulled on a white T-shirt and black shorts. He didn't look up.

'The audit?' she asked, walking over to him. 'Anything interesting?'

'Depends if you find the sepsis resus care-pathway interesting or not.'

'Well, of course it's interesting,' she replied, dragging a chair to sit alongside him. 'Anything we can do to help with the early detection of sepsis has got to be interesting. What does the audit show?'

'Compliance with the Sepsis Six protocol is good but I'm setting a goal of one hundred per cent compliance. There's no reason we can't achieve that.'

'Is it all six of the interventions we're not compliant with or just one of them?'

'We're one hundred per cent with monitoring output, giving oxygen and starting fluids, but less with taking blood cultures, measuring lactate and starting antibiotics. It's nearly there but I won't settle for anything less than perfect. Doing those things in that first hour after admission increases survival rate significantly.'

'We'll need to organise some training sessions with the staff to remind them about the importance of completing all six parts of the protocol. I can speak to the comms team to see if we can have a month where the screen saver on all department computers and devices highlights the protocol. Staff will see the messaging every time they log on or even walk past a screen. What do you think?'

'I think that's an excellent idea.'

'Great, I'll get on it as soon as we get back.'

He nodded just a touch, watchful eyes lingering silently, not leaving hers, sending a searing heat blazing through her. Was this a night to make up for lost time?

Did he want her as she wanted him?

He lowered his gaze, returning to his laptop. No; he'd turned away, back to his work.

'Apparently, it's perfectly acceptable to sleep in the same bed with someone you're not married to as long as you both keep one foot on the floor,' she said, standing and dragging her chair back to its original position, hoping her voice sounded lighter and more in control than she felt.

'I'll sleep on the sofa,' replied Dexter, not looking up.

He definitely wasn't interested.

'Don't be silly; you'll have a bad back tomorrow if you do that. Don't worry, I don't bite.' She clamped her mouth shut but it was too late…the words had been said. She was glad he had his back to her.

Where had that come from?

If he was happy to sleep on the sofa, then that was probably the best option. *He* might well have found a T-shirt, but she didn't have anything that would double up as nightwear. Did she want to be naked in the same bed as Dexter Stevens?

Hell, yes.

No way.

Talk about a dilemma…

'I'll be fine—I've slept in worse places.'

'Have you? Where?'

'The doctors' mess is much worse.'

Tilly laughed, relieved he'd ignored her errant comment about not biting.

Dexter turned his head to look at her. 'I'm not joking.'

'It's not that bad. At least there's a bed.'

He didn't react but turned back to his work. She sat down on the end of the bed watching him from behind as he tapped away, dark head bent. His white T-shirt clung to every dip and curve of his muscles. He stopped typing and sat up straighter, stretching his arms high above his head, grasping one elbow and then the other, stretching more deeply, his muscles flexing beautifully. She picked up her phone.

'I'll set an alarm for eight... Breakfast is from seven thirty and the wedding ceremony starts at eleven.'

'Mm-hmm.'

'I think I'll go to bed now, then.'

'Mm-hmm.'

If she was looking for riveting conversation, then Dexter Stevens was definitely the wrong guy. The only time he engaged was when he was talking shop and, what with the emergency tracheotomy in the castle courtyard and the Sepsis Six protocol, she was done with talking shop for this evening.

'Will you be long?' Tilly pulled back the duvet on the bed and undid the tie on the bath robe.

'No idea. Don't wait for me, though.'

She let the bathrobe fall to the floor and slid into bed, pulling up the duvet even though, really, it was too warm for it. Was he going to get into bed? What would she do if he did? Lachlan leaving the scene like a bat out of hell after her telling him about her leukaemia had taught her many things—one of which was that, if she ever found herself being drawn towards another man, he would either have to be a short-term bit of fun or absolutely be able to handle her medical past.

She was drawn to Dexter Stevens. And he didn't do fun. Neither would he be the kind of solid, understanding, empathic support she wanted from someone. In fact, he was everything she didn't want in a man, so why was her heart banging so hard in her chest that she was sure he'd be able to hear it?

Tilly lifted her head and punched her pillow before resting back on it again. Dexter was still apparently deep in concentration. She peered at him from over the top of the duvet and her heart-rate notched up. His dark silhouette was enhanced by the glow from the angle-poise lamp.

He wanted to sleep on the sofa. *Was she disappointed?* She should be relieved, really. She knew nothing about him. She didn't know if he had family, where he was from, what he enjoyed doing outside of work or if he had any longer-term plans and goals—nothing, *nada*, *niente*. He was a closed book. And that was a good reason to stay well clear of him.

It was also the reason he intrigued her.

Like a beautifully wrapped gift found hidden at the back of a mum's wardrobe just before Christmas, Dexter was a deliciously mysterious, forbidden secret. She knew she shouldn't feel it, but she couldn't help that his very mystery lured her towards him and made her want to peel back the wrapping paper to take a peek at what was inside.

CHAPTER SEVEN

TILLY OPENED FIRST one eye and then the other. The room was dark and, lifting herself up onto her elbows, she looked around as her eyes adjusted. Chinks of daylight slanted through the edges of the heavy curtains at the windows, lighting the blanket-covered and still-sleeping body of Dexter on the sofa a few feet away. She could just make out his rhythmic breathing.

Sitting up, she reached for the over-sized bath robe she'd dropped onto the floor last night. It would have been a mistake to risk being in the same bed together—Lord knew what would have happened, and where would that have left her? Potentially embroiled in another relationship with a wholly unsuitable, emotionally void man.

Lowering her feet to the floor, she stood, pulling the sash tightly around her waist. She'd have a nice shower, get some breakfast and enjoy the wedding—that was why she was here, after all, not to end up in bed with a man who didn't come anywhere near ticking any of her boxes.

Treading stealthily across the carpet towards the bathroom, Tilly didn't take a breath. She wanted to lock the door and get into the shower before he awoke—she wasn't going to have a repeat of yesterday. But a floorboard creaked as she trod on it, bringing her to a halt. She swung round, looking back towards the sofa. Dexter moved and the blanket he'd covered himself with fell to the floor with a soft thud.

Her errant gaze slid down his body—he was naked apart from his boxer shorts. Her pulse quickened and she closed her eyes, scolding herself for looking. When she opened them again, he was wide awake and looking at her, the blanket still on the floor. She gasped. Her instinct was to bolt for the bathroom and slam shut the door but her feet seemed to be stuck to the floor.

'Morning,' she managed.

Dexter swung himself upright, yawning and stretching his arms high above his head before leaning to pick up the blanket.

'Morning,' he replied.

'Good job you don't sleep completely naked.' The words were out before she'd even thought them, and her fingers and toes curled.

'Quite.'

She nodded towards the blanket, which now lay beside him on the sofa. 'With the blanket falling off, I mean.'

He glanced at the blanket.

'Don't worry, I haven't taken photos for the notice board at work.'

She smiled, knowing full well it was probably the most awkward smile in the world. What the hell had happened to her mouth? Could she make this any worse?

Stop talking, Tilly.

Dexter's eyes widened. 'Thanks for that.'

'Right, well, I think I'll get a shower.'

'Okay.'

Heart hammering, she managed not to run to the bathroom, but when she got there she locked the door, turned on the shower and stepped under the warm water, her face turned upwards and relief flooding through her that she was no longer standing before an almost naked Dexter, who must be wondering what on earth had got into her. But she knew exactly what had got into her. She'd seen more of his heavenly body in the last twenty-four hours than she could ever have dared to hope…and it had sent common sense running for the hills.

Damn this room mix-up.

At least she only had one more night to get through and she could manage that without being tempted again by him…surely?

Dexter went over to the window to pull back the heavy curtains and flood the room with bright, early-morning summer sunshine. He looked over to the bed she'd slept in—the bed they both could have slept in. It was a crumpled mess and he instinctively reached for the duvet to straighten it. The sheet was still warm and he withdrew his hand, as though it had burned him. Suddenly it seemed too intimate to touch her bed linen.

Watching her to check she'd fallen asleep last night before he'd tried to make himself comfortable on the sofa had also been too intimate. She'd

94 WEDDING FLING TO FOREVER

been spread out like a starfish under the duvet, her ebony and amethyst hair fanning out over the pillow, her lips parted slightly, her breaths long, deep and contented.

What if he'd accepted her invitation to share it with her? He'd never shared a bed with a woman platonically. And that was what she'd invited him to do, with the whole 'one foot on the floor' suggestion. But he hadn't trusted himself and he hadn't trusted that erotic fiery gleam in her eyes last night when she'd caught him in the shower either. Tilly wasn't a one-night stand sort of woman. She deserved better than that. She deserved better than him. He wasn't a match for her. He knew what he was—an uptight, hard-boiled, frosty loner and he didn't want her spirit crushed by that.

'All yours,' said Tilly, walking across the bedroom and opening the wardrobe. 'I'm going down to breakfast, so I'll see you down there.' She glanced out of the window as she passed. 'Gorgeous day for it.'

'Sure,' he replied. 'Yes.'

She wasn't waiting for him, then. Just as well. They were colleagues and he'd do well to start trying to remember that. Anyway, he didn't want to see that gleam in her eyes again. It was way too tempting.

Tilly nudged his arm. He looked down to where she pointed at in the small brochure provided for guests who'd not been to a south Indian wedding before, which explained each step in the ceremony.

'This is the most important bit,' she whispered, her eyes gleaming with excitement, as usual making him not want to look away.

The guests were sitting in the courtyard of the castle. A beautifully ornate mandap had been erected as an altar and was decorated with flowers and mango and banana leaves, under which the bride, groom and wedding party sat on golden, flower-covered chairs, almost like thrones. The scene was one of vibrant, sunny, jewel colours and the guests were all dressed brightly, many of them in traditional Indian robes of beautiful, opulent fabrics.

Dexter glanced back at Tilly, who sat beside him watching the elaborate ceremony, clearly enthralled. She wore a traditional sari of a deep pink and orange and edged with a pattern in golden thread. He looked down at her small hands which she held in her lap. The henna she'd had done last night had darkened into a rich red-brown colour, the design intricate and quite beautiful. The lulling chanting of the priest grew louder, making Dexter look back at the bride and groom who stood from their thrones and began to walk round the dish of sacred fire in the centre of the mandap.

Suddenly, Tilly's hand was on his forearm. 'The seven steps,' she whispered excitedly, not looking at him.

He smiled, dropping his head as he did so. Why did she make him want to smile so much? She had an enchanting, childlike quality about her sometimes that did that to him. He didn't like weddings and usually did everything in his power to avoid them. Why two people, logical in every other aspect of their lives, could make such an illogical decision as tying themselves together for ever, he just couldn't fathom. How could two people ever be so 'right' together that they'd risk their whole future on each other? Why would anyone want to bare their soul to another person, let them know everything about you, be judged, chewed up and spat out by them?

Tilly released his arm and held her hands clasped together at her chest. She drew in a deep breath and watched the scene in front of them. The bride and groom threw rice, herbs and flowers into the sacred fire, making the flames momentarily flare higher.

He glanced down at the order of service—Dhanya Homam, offerings to Agni, the god of fire, to solidify the bond between their two families. He glanced at all the players on the stage—both sets of parents were beaming, looking happy and proud, and he caught a look between the groom and his father that stilled his heart. A smile from son to father, a returning smile and a slight nod from father to son—an acknowledgement, an understanding, passing between them—mutual love, pride, respect and a warm, trusting bond strengthened over the years.

Family. He'd never had a family. He'd imagined what it might have been like if he had, though. His young mind had invented a mother he'd never known. She'd have been warm, kind and smiling; she'd have hugged him when he'd come home from school, cook meals for him and read him bedtime stories. She'd have been there when he lost his first tooth, won races at sports day and graduated from medical school.

She'd have loved him. He'd fallen asleep at night, willing what he could only imagine to come true, wishing he'd known her. But he'd never woken up in the morning to see her in the kitchen making breakfast, slipping a box of sandwiches into his school bag for lunch or kissing him on the top of his head as he left for school. Instead he'd awoken each day wondering which version of his father would be there—the one who had passed out on the sofa surrounded by bottles, cans and cigarette ends or the one who would try to help him with his homework.

He closed his eyes, squeezing them shut, willing away the sights and sounds of those days. His father's red, angry face swam into view, his mouth moving, shouting at him, a shower of beer-smelling spittle splattering into his young face. Instinctively he moved backwards, away from it, his eyes snapping open, his breathing deeper, his fingers gripping the order of service.

Suddenly there was applause. Everyone was clapping and the wedding party stood in a line at the front, all beaming smiles as the photographer clicked away. Tilly nudged him with her elbow and frowned at him, nodding towards his hands. He joined in the applause as the happy couple began to make their way back down the aisle between the rows of clapping guests.

'Wasn't that gorgeous?' said Tilly, looking as

98   WEDDING FLING TO FOREVER

though she'd won the lottery. 'They look so fabulous and so happy.'

He knew what he was supposed to say. 'They do; very happy.' She was right. The difference was that she felt it and he didn't. Years of careful programming not to succumb to the danger of allowing feelings into his life had made sure of that.

They filed down the aisle with the other guests, Tilly taking a handful of flower petals from a bowl on a table.

'Take some,' she instructed.

He sighed. Hadn't his duty been done now? He'd turned up to the wedding and they were married now. Wasn't that enough?

'Go on,' said Tilly, nodding towards the bowl. 'Don't be a party pooper.'

He took a handful of petals. 'What are we supposed to do with these?'

'Make tea with them,' she replied, rolling her eyes. 'What do you think we do with them?'

He stared at her. 'I expect we do the entirely illogical thing and toss them at the newlyweds, creating a mess for someone else to clear up later?'

She pursed her lips. 'Not everything has to be logical, Dexter.'

'The world would be a far better place if people were more logical and less governed so much by their emotions.'

She looked at him, puzzled. 'I think you actually mean that.'

Of course he did. Emotions completely messed up

COLETTE COOPER 99

logical decision making and turned normal people into defenceless victims.

'Ready, everyone?' the photographer called.

'Come on, party pooper,' said Tilly. 'Come and throw your illogical petals and pretend as if you're happy to be here.'

He wasn't happy to be here. *Was he?* He was happy to be with Tilly.

'On three,' called the photographer, as everyone held their hands aloft and poised, ready for the staged 'spontaneous' throwing of petals. 'One... two...three!'

Brightly coloured flower petals rained down on the newlyweds, who ducked, dodged and laughed as the guests cheered and the photographer captured the moment.

'They look so happy,' said Tilly. 'Shall we go and check on Grandpa again, now the ceremony is done?'

Geetha's grandpa had been discharged from hospital after the emergency tracheostomy yesterday, only on the basis that Dexter would be around. He'd spoken to the ENT consultant on the phone and assured him that he'd monitor him so that the old man could see his granddaughter get married.

'Fancy a walk on the beach before the meal, while the photographer is doing her thing?' said Tilly, taking a sip of champagne.

'I might go back to the room and finish my audit.'

'No! On a day like this? It's a wedding, it's a glorious summer's day and the beach is just down there.

You can't go and sit in a hotel room and do a stuffy old audit like a complete Grinch. Come on, drink up. Let's check on Grandpa and go to the beach.'

Geetha was bending down and hugging her grandpa, who was sitting in the wheelchair the hospital had provided so that he could attend the wedding. 'Here he is,' she said, beaming as she stood and saw Dexter approaching. 'Our hero.'

Dexter cringed. He didn't need a whole new round of awkward hugs and slaps on the back. He directed his attention to his patient, squatting on his haunches beside his wheelchair.

'How are you doing?'

Tilly stood beside him.

Geetha's grandpa nodded, smiling, but Dexter noticed a slight ashen pallor to his skin, which concerned him.

'I'm just going to check your pulse,' he said, reaching for Grandpa's wrist. It was a little fast but steady. If they'd been in hospital, he'd have had an array of medical equipment to hand. As it was, he was glad he'd requested that the local hospital send some kit to the castle instead.

'Everything okay?' said Geetha, frowning.

'I'm going to do a proper examination,' said Dexter. 'Inside, with the equipment from the hospital.' He looked at Grandpa. 'Is that okay with you?' The old man nodded in agreement.

'I'll come with you,' said Tilly, taking the handles of the wheelchair and kicking off the break.

'May I come too?' said the patient's wife.

'Of course,' replied Tilly. 'It's just the normal checks we'd run after doing a tracheostomy, don't worry.'

'I'll come too,' said Geetha, but Tilly touched her arm.

'It's your wedding day,' said Tilly. 'We'll be back before you've even missed us, and Dexter will update you straight away.'

Dexter collected the equipment from a store-room, confirming with the receptionist that they could use one of the adjoining offices as a makeshift examination room. The tracheostomy yesterday had been performed as an emergency, using less than ideal equipment and in less than ideal circumstances. They'd avoided the immediate complications of bleeding, tracheal rupture and laryngeal nerve damage, but there were other issues that could come a little further down the line, and that was what concerned him right now.

Tilly joined him in the store room.

'What's worrying you?' she asked, her voice lowered.

'Infection.'

She grimaced. 'It's a distinct possibility, isn't it, with it being done how it was? It wasn't exactly a sterile procedure.'

'Exactly. I want to check his sats and temperature and have a look at the wound.'

'Sounds like a plan.' Tilly pushed open the door to the makeshift surgery. 'We're back,' she said to

102   WEDDING FLING TO FOREVER

the grandparents, who were holding hands as they sat side by side.

Dexter took the oxygen saturation probe out of its box, putting it on one of his fingers to test it before placing it on the patient. Portable probes these days were as accurate and reliable as those in hospitals, and he was confident this one would do the job. Tilly pulled out a tympanic thermometer and explained what she was doing before she inserted it lightly into Grandpa's ear. It beeped a few seconds later.

'Thirty-eight,' she announced, brightly, not giving away that the figure was concerning. She was clearly as aware as Dexter that Geetha's grandparents gaze was on them, watching for any signs that there was a concern. No need to worry them. This was likely an infection due to the lack of sterile equipment when he'd had to perform the procedure. He'd have been lucky not to develop an infection, really.

Dexter glanced at the probe on the man's finger.

'Sats fine at ninety-eight; heart rate ninety. I'm just going to have a quick look at the neck wound, if that's okay?'

Tilly had already opened a sterile pack, laying it on the desk. He donned the gloves. Tilly had already done the same and proceeded to remove the tracheostomy dressing ready for him to inspect it. He could have managed this examination on his own, but having her there with him, knowing how competent she was, added a level of reassurance that was oddly agreeable.

With the stoma site exposed, it was easy to see

that he'd been right in thinking that their patient's symptoms added up to there being an infection at the incision site. It was disappointing, but not unexpected. Tilly had poured some saline solution into a small sterile pot and he dipped some sterile gauze into it, swabbing around the tracheostomy site before drying it and applying a fresh dressing.

'I think a short course of antibiotics would be advisable,' he said, pulling off his gloves and dropping them back into the opened pack. 'Perfectly normal after a procedure like this.'

'I'm sure I noticed a pharmacy in the village,' said Tilly. 'We can pop down and pick them up for you.'

'That's very kind,' said Geetha's grandma. 'Thank you…both of you.'

They took the steps down to the village from the castle. They were quite steep and Tilly needed to lift the fabric of her sari with one hand and hold onto Dexter's arm with the other. She didn't ask if she could take his arm; she just held onto it as if it was the most natural thing in the world to do.

Suddenly, out of nowhere, a golden retriever came bounding towards them.

'Hello, girl,' said Dexter, taking hold of the dog's collar and glancing round, looking for an owner.

'Sorry,' said an older man, jogging up to them and panting a little. 'She slipped her lead.'

Dexter crouched beside the dog, ruffling her ears. 'You're all right, aren't you, girl? Just excited to be off your lead and on a run.' He took the lead from

104 WEDDING FLING TO FOREVER

the man and reattached it, handing it over to him. 'She's gorgeous.' He smiled at the dog, still stroking her.

'She can be a bit of a rogue,' her owner replied. 'But, yes, she's a good girl…most of the time. Sorry, anyway—I'll leave you two in peace.'

'You've made a friend there,' said Tilly, watching him as he got to his feet.

'Dogs will befriend anyone who's kind to them,' he replied as they continued the walk into the village. 'And they're way less complicated than humans.'

His relationship with dogs was the only relationship he trusted. They were the only ones who'd never let him down; the only ones he could rely on come rain or shine. They were non-judgmental, unprejudiced and completely logical. Dog relationships were simple, safe and predictable. Human relationships were the exact opposite.

'You're probably right there,' said Tilly, laughing. 'Here's the pharmacy.'

Dexter wrote out the prescription for the antibiotics and they took them back to the castle, ensuring that Geetha's grandpa started the course immediately and keeping a close eye on him for the rest of the afternoon. To their relief, a repeat temperature check later on after the meal indicated that his condition was stable.

CHAPTER EIGHT

DEXTER WANTED TO RUN…or hide…but he wasn't really in a position to do either. He had to go to the party; of course he did. He was in a senior position in the hospital and was required to attend the wedding of another very senior member of staff, whom he did actually like and respect. In addition, Tilly clearly wasn't going to let him off the hook, so his hands were tied but, hell, he'd do almost anything not to go. Perhaps he could just leave early.

'Ready?' said Tilly as he came out of the bathroom.

He drew in a breath. She wore a midnight-blue silk dress that cinched in at her waist and flowed to the floor, shimmering like the dark waters of the deep ocean. The colour accentuated beautifully her ebony hair and porcelain skin, which seemed to have an almost ethereal glow. She held a silver chain with the outline of a heart at her neck, which nestled just above her cleavage.

His body reacted instinctively. He swallowed. 'You look lovely.' The words escaped his lips before he'd even realised he'd thought them.

She curtsied, smiling. 'Thank you…and you don't look too bad yourself. Would you fasten this for me?'

He took a step towards her and she turned, still holding onto the ends of the necklace. Moving her hair to one side, he took the ends of the chain from her fingers, trying not to touch her skin but desperately wanting to. If he touched her, even lightly, he wouldn't want to let go.

The evening was warm. Beautifully decorated tables were dotted around the green, and guests were mingling, chinking glasses, finding their place names and sitting down. The hum of amiable chatter fused with music playing softly from the speakers. Dexter took a sparkling water from the tray a waiter offered him and Tilly opted for champagne. They'd been seated at the same table, but apart, and Dexter missed her presence beside him; missed having her smile all to himself. He answered questions put to him by the guests next to him but found his gaze kept wandering back to Tilly, who was chatting as easily as she always did, laughing and making those around her laugh with her.

There was an announcement from the DJ to gather round the dance floor, as the bride and groom were about to have their first dance. Dexter watched from the back of the crowd and spotted Tilly right at the front, beaming with delight as the couple swayed and twirled to the song before beckoning everyone else to join them. Tilly was the first onto the dance floor, arms in the air, laughing with the others who'd also joined in until the floor was crowded.

He glanced around. Everyone was either eating, drinking, dancing, chatting or laughing. The atmosphere was one of happy, good-natured revelry but he still felt a tightness in his gut. He knew only too well how apparently good-natured fun could so quickly and easily change into something quite different. A crack and a hiss behind him made his jaw clench harder—the opening of a can was an all too familiar sound from childhood, one which had usually signalled an evening of unruly, rowdy behaviour, coarse jokes, cursing, arguments and sometimes worse.

A couple of men walked past him to get to the dance floor and one bumped into his shoulder, making his drink slosh and spill slightly.

'Sorry, mate.'

Dexter nodded. He'd learned to put up with worse. He'd learned not to answer back when his father had shouted at him for no good reason; not to ask why there was no dinner money for school or why they couldn't turn on a radiator in the winter. He'd learned to accept in silence whatever had been thrown at him when his father was drunk. Doing otherwise had been futile…and dangerous. He'd mastered the art of lying about the bruises.

There had been a huge, old oak tree in a park that he used to climb—it had been a great place to hide from the world and find some peace and stillness. That old oak tree had not only given him shelter from the raging storm that had been his father, it had also provided him with plausible reasons for the regular bruises and probably prevented him from being taken into care.

Tilly made her way through the crowd and stood on the edge of the dance floor, still dancing and beckoning for him to join her. He shook his head

108 WEDDING FLING TO FOREVER

but she continued to beckon him, pretending to look crestfallen. The last thing he wanted to do was to get onto that dance floor; in fact, he didn't even want to be here. He wanted to be up in the safe, secure branches of his oak tree.

Someone reached for Tilly's arm, spinning her round, and she shimmied her way back into the crowd of dancers and was lost. Relief washed over him. He needed to get away. He made his way away from the lights, music and revelry and walked towards the castle walls and coastal path.

'Dexter! Where are you going?'

Tilly. He turned around. The sight of her walking towards him in the twilight, the breeze playing with her hair and the soft fabric of her dress, moulding it against her body, pulled every breath of air from his lungs. She caught up with him and fell into step beside him.

'I haven't seen the coastal path yet.' He hoped his voice sounded normal because he sure as hell didn't feel normal—the strength of his response to this woman, the deeply unsettling effect she had on his pulse, defied all logical reasoning. He needed time on his own; time to work out how he was going to deal with having to spend another night with her in that room without making a move he'd regret.

'Can I come?'

'Not in those.' He nodded to her feet, upon which were high-heeled, strappy sandals. 'You go and enjoy the party.'

'I'd rather be with you.'

COLETTE COOPER 109

Dexter stopped walking and stared at her.

Rather be with him when she was the life and soul of the party and lived to be around other people and have fun?

'If we go to the beach instead of along the coastal path, I can take my sandals off and go barefoot.'

She wanted to be with him.

And he wanted to be with her...even more than he didn't.

'If you're sure?'

'I'm certain,' said Tilly. 'What could be nicer than an evening stroll along the beach as the sun goes down?'

They descended the stone steps to the beach. She kicked off her sandals, swinging them by the straps as they walked, then she stopped, turning to him and grinning. He knew that grin.

'Race you to the sea,' she said, picking up her dress. She began running, looking behind her and laughing. 'Come on, Dexter.'

He looked down at his feet. He wore black patent dress shoes, completely unsuitable for running in the sand. But he wanted to follow her, to run barefoot with her towards the roar of the ocean on this wild, beautiful, Northumbrian beach. He'd never run barefoot across sand. He'd never been coaxed to do it by a beautiful, clever, funny, warm-hearted woman with sparkling eyes, the brightest smile and amethyst coloured hair.

But he wanted to nonetheless.

What was she doing to him? This went against ev-

WEDDING FLING TO FOREVER

erything he knew to be right. What had happened to his mantra of keeping his distance, keeping illogical emotions out of it and staying in control?

'Come on, Dexter!'

She turned round again, her hair blowing in the breeze. She captured some of it, tucking it behind her ear, but it whipped back into her face. He was powerless to resist her.

'Last one in the sea has to sleep on the sofa tonight.' She started skipping backwards, still looking at him, holding up the ocean blue fabric of her evening dress, her warm laughter carried away by the breeze.

Dexter squatted on his haunches, undid his laces, kicked off his shoes and socks and began to jog towards her, not quite believing what he was doing. Tilly squealed, turned on her heel and ran headlong for the sea. He caught up with her easily and she turned to him as they ran alongside each other, his heart responding to the exertion, but singing too. Why had he never done this before? *Because no one like Tilly had ever asked him.*

'Don't let me win,' she called, a little breathlessly.

'You don't mind sleeping on the sofa tonight?'

'I'm not going to be sleeping on the sofa.'

'Unless I let you win, you will be.'

Tilly laughed, hitching her dress up higher, picking up the pace and speeding ahead. He caught up but jogged alongside her, not wanting to race ahead and lose sight of her. The sand beneath his feet began to change from soft, dry and powdery to cooler and damp as they neared the edge of the water; the crash of the waves grew louder and the breeze stronger. Tilly ducked as a squawking seagull swooped in front of them, making her laugh as if she didn't have a care in the world.

The pace of his heart picked up and it was more than obvious it wasn't entirely due to the physical exertion of running headlong into the wind. He could have run flat out on a treadmill on an incline and it wouldn't have felt the same as it did jogging easily alongside Tilly. It wasn't the running that made his heart thump hard in his chest—it was being with her.

Tilly gathered her dress up higher as she reached the sea at the exact same moment he did. 'It's freezing,' she shrieked, hopping from one foot to the other and darting back out again.

She was right, it was. And he'd completely neglected to hitch up his trousers, which were now soaking wet from the knees down.

She pointed at them, laughing. 'You should have taken them off with your socks and shoes, Dexter,' she called over the sound of the waves, doubled over laughing and catching her breath.

He should have. Logic should have warned him. But when Tilly had hitched up her dress in one hand, held her sandals in the other and run laughing, headlong towards the sea, calling to him, logic hadn't been in charge.

'At least I can't go back to the party now,' he said, squeezing some of the water from his trousers.

112 WEDDING FLING TO FOREVER

They began walking back up the beach towards the castle.

'Why do you dislike parties so much?'

He closed his eyes, opened them and studiously avoided looking at her. *Don't, Tilly.*

'It's a huge expanse of beach, isn't it?'

'It is, but that doesn't answer my question.'

Should he open up a little, as she obviously wanted him to? *What would happen if he did?*

He sensed danger.

No, keep it light.

'I guess your assessment of me is correct—I'm just a Grinchy, sourpuss party pooper.' He smiled, hoping it looked genuine and light-hearted, but guessing it wouldn't. 'It's still pretty warm, isn't it?'

'But you're not, Dexter. You're not really at all like the character you'd have everyone believe you are.' She grinned. 'Your trousers are testament to that. And you care about people; you always do your absolute best for patients. And look at how you were with that dog earlier—she adored you. And dogs are very intuitive—they can sense the good in people.'

'Dogs accept people as they are,' he replied. 'They don't have hidden agendas. If you're good to them, they simply accept it. Unfortunately, people aren't like that, which is why I try to hang around with dogs more than I do people.' He smiled, again hoping to keep the conversation light.

'You pretend not to care; why do you do that?'

This was getting way too deep for his liking but

she wasn't giving up. She was probing him for answers, pushing his boundaries. He didn't like it.

Then give her something...a little nugget of information to satisfy her curiosity, something she couldn't make anything out of; something innocuous.

'Have I told you I volunteer at Battersea Dogs' and Cats' Home?'

Her eyes widened. 'Do you? Wow.'

He frowned. *Why was that so hard to believe?*

'Why "wow"?'

She blinked. 'Well, I just never…'

'Well, I do…a few times a week, whenever I get chance.' He felt slightly affronted by her surprise.

'Well, that's great; how lovely. You must really enjoy it.'

'I do and I'm not sure why you sound so surprised. I do have a life outside of the hospital, you know.'

'Of course you do.' She gave him a sidelong glance, her lips curving into a smile as she looked at him from beneath lowered lashes, making his stomach clench. 'I just imagined you spending your time at the gym or running, or something like that.'

He didn't reply.

Why did she look at him in that way? She was all sassy challenge one moment and coy seduction the next. His head was spinning.

'I manage both, and one or two other things too.'

'But not parties.'

He stopped walking and turned to face her.

'No.'

'Pity.'

He frowned. 'Why?'

Tilly opened her arms wide. 'Because I think you'd enjoy yourself. You just need to let go a little.'

'I don't like letting go.'

She gave that look again—she looked at him from underneath those luscious, dark lashes and her lips went into that barely there but totally sensuous pout. It was a look that made his stomach clench and all rational thought disappear from his mind.

'Oh, but I think you do, Dexter… You've just run headlong into the sea fully clothed.'

He raised an eyebrow, trying to ignore the fact that his heart was suddenly trying to break out of his chest. He started walking again.

'I have the distinct impression that lurking beneath that cool, buttoned-up mask, there is the possibility of endless fun.' It was almost dark but he could see the gleam in her eyes. 'Come back to the party, Dexter; let yourself go. It doesn't matter if you can't dance; no one will care if you make a fool of yourself.'

But *he* cared. He didn't want to let go. And the burning embarrassment he'd felt as a child when he'd tried to fit in with his father's friends and ended up throwing up in front of them all, making a fool of himself, still stung. He wasn't making a fool of himself again by trying to please.

'Tilly, if you want to go back to the party, please feel free, but I just don't like being in rowdy places with crowds of drunken revellers, that's all; it's just not my thing, okay?' He didn't want this conversation.

'It's not a rowdy, drunken party, Dexter, it's a wedding reception.'

'Same thing.'

'You're such a—'

'Stop it!' said Dexter, turning to face her. 'Stop telling me what a spoilsport I am. If you want to go to the party, please go, but don't try to force me into being in an environment I've tried to avoid all my life.' He hated himself immediately for raising his voice to her. 'I'm sorry.'

'What happened to you, Dexter?' Her voice was soft, luring and beckoning him as if towards a safe harbour in a storm…a harbour he'd been searching for his whole life. He lifted his gaze, met her soft, kind, amethyst eyes and was lost. Gorgeous, lovely, enchanting Tilly had said she wanted to be with him. And she wanted to know about him. Because she cared.

'My father used to like a lot of parties…' The words came out of nowhere, surprising him.

She looked at him, holding his gaze, giving him time and space, allowing him to speak or not.

'They always involved a lot of alcohol.'

She closed her eyes slowly before opening them again and fixing her gaze back on him. She was beginning to understand. And, somehow, he wanted to tell her more. But people didn't want to hear about his pain, not really; that was why he kept quiet about

116 WEDDING FLING TO FOREVER

it. That and because he couldn't even begin to find the words to explain he'd ruined his family, caused his father to seek solace in drink and killed his own mother by being born.

How could he tell her that? Tilly was so in tune with other people and their feelings; so full of empathy and compassion. She'd be full of pity for him... and that was the last thing he wanted. Pity wasn't going to erase what had happened. He'd answer her question, in part, but he wasn't going to tell her everything.

'Don't get me wrong—he wasn't all bad. When he was sober, he could be good, kind—fun, even. It's just that didn't happen very often. Most of his wages went on booze, leaving very little for food, clothes, heating... Then, when he lost his job for being drunk at work, there was even less to go around. He spent most of his time either at the pub, round at his mates' places or at home, drinking.'

She nodded slowly, looking sombre. 'I see.'

But she didn't...not yet. 'Alcohol has different effects on different people, doesn't it? We see it all the time in A&E. Some people are merry and fun, some become morose and others become aggressive and violent. My father was in the latter category.'

'Oh, Dexter...'

He began walking again. He didn't want pity but he did want her to know that about him, for some reason. He wanted shelter from the storm...just for a moment.

'I survived...my father didn't. He died of liver

failure a few years ago.' He knew he sounded cold, but it was a fact; a cold, hard fact, simple as that.

'What about your mum?'

'She died.' He couldn't say the words which would explain any more than that. He couldn't tell her that her death had been his fault, neither could he say the words out loud that he'd known were true for so long—that his father's drinking had probably been his fault too. His father had most likely sought solace in alcohol to help him forget that his only son had killed his wife.

'Dexter, I'm so sorry.' Tilly had stopped walking but he carried on, not wanting to see the sympathy he knew would be there in her beautiful eyes. He wasn't one of her patients. When she caught up with him, she touched his arm and he flinched, but she held on to him, making him stop and turn towards her.

'I don't need pity, Tilly. It's a period in my life I'd rather forget. I'm over it. It just means that I don't like alcohol-fuelled parties, that's all.'

'Okay, no sympathy.' She held up her palms in surrender. 'Not for adult Dexter. But allow me to have a little for young Dexter.'

He frowned. 'Bit late for that.'

But Tilly looked up into his eyes and he could do nothing but surrender to her gaze. 'I wish I could have been there to stop what happened to you.'

Dexter swallowed. No one had ever spoken to him like this.

'Thank you.' His voice was thick and he didn't trust himself to say anything else.

'I know you're not a huggy person, but a hug might help.' She smiled at him tentatively, almost shyly, and he nodded. Wrapping her arms around his waist, she drew him in close, squeezing him, resting her head against his chest as he closed his arms around her.

He'd never learned how to be hugged and it had always felt alien, awkward, something other people did—people who'd grown up in loving families. He didn't want to let her go, didn't want to leave the safe, warm harbour, but he broke the embrace, still unable to trust himself to speak.

'Should we head back before the sun sets completely?' asked Tilly. 'We don't need to go to the party.'

Dexter nodded, unable to look at her. They began walking back up the beach side by side, their hands accidentally brushing each other's on occasion. It would have been so easy to reach for her but that would mean admitting things to himself that he wasn't ready to admit.

CHAPTER NINE

'Let's go up to the battery terrace,' said Tilly. 'The sunset over the sea will be stunning from up there. I love being by the sea; it's why Australia is where I want to be.'

'You want to go on holiday there?'

'I want to *live* there,' she replied, looking at him quizzically.

Dexter stopped walking and stared at her incredulously. '*Live* there?'

'Of course.' She laughed. 'How am I going to work there if I don't live there?'

'You're going to *work* there?'

'Yes.'

He didn't know. But he wouldn't, would he? He didn't listen to chatter, didn't care about what was going on in people's lives and wasn't interested in making friends.

'I didn't know.'

'Sorry, I just thought you did. Everyone else does.'

'Well, don't hold your breath,' he replied. 'It can take months.'

'I applied over a year ago.'

'Have you registered with the nursing board?'

'Yes.'

'Passed the exams?'

'The qualifications I have already mean I don't

120 WEDDING FLING TO FOREVER

need to sit any. There's just an orientation programme when I get there.'

'Have you applied for a visa?'

'Already got it.'

'Which visa?'

'It's an employer-sponsored one.'

'So you have a job lined up?'

Tilly clasped her hands in front of her excitedly. 'Only in an A&E within a ten-minute walk of Bondi Beach—how amazing is that?'

He stared at her a moment longer then began walking again. 'Excellent…really excellent. I'm pleased for you…if that's what you want.'

But something in his tone told her he didn't mean what he'd said and there was now space between them as they walked that hadn't been there on the way up from the beach, when she'd been able to feel the warmth of his skin as it had brushed her own.

They came to the edge of the battlement with its distinctively shaped merlons where huge, black canons stood in the crenels between them, pointing out to sea, fending off would-be intruders from breaching the walls.

'Wow,' said Tilly, standing beside Dexter and leaning on the cool stone. 'Look at the colours in that sky. It's so dramatic and mystical; a dreamy symphony of colour as the sun prepares to sleep and the day surrenders to the dark night.'

'It's actually because the shorter blue colourwavelengths of light are scattered off particles in the atmosphere when the sun is lower, letting the red and orange wavelengths become more visible, hence the reds, oranges and pinks you can see.'

Tilly scowled at him.

'What?' said Dexter, looking puzzled.

'You just ruined it.'

'Ruined what?'

'The awe-inspiring romance and magic of a beautiful sunset.'

'By explaining the science behind it?'

'Yes—it's a very Grinchy thing to do.'

'Science can still be awe-inspiring.'

'It can't be romantic and magical, though, can it?'

He looked at her, his cobalt eyes reflecting the golden embers of the sinking sun, a slight frown creasing his brow. Her heart picked up its pace and that now familiar-heat at his proximity flooded through her. He was so near—close enough to touch—but also so far away. This *could* have been romantic. If he wasn't such a cold fish.

'Is that what you want?' he asked.

'What do you mean?'

'Romance?' he replied. 'Magic?'

His face was a composed mask but his eyes held hers with a blazing intensity that jolted her pulse into overdrive.

'Isn't that what everyone wants?'

Where was this going?

'I'm probably not the right person to ask.'

Tilly let out a breath. Of course he wasn't. Dexter saw everything in black and white. Everything was science and logic and things that weren't…well, they weren't worth bothering with.

'Why not?' she asked, watching him, her head tilted to one side. She wanted to know. What made Dexter Stevens tick? But he broke their shared gaze and looked out to sea.

'I don't believe in happy-ever-afters.'

'Oh, don't say that. We're at a wedding—we're right in the middle of a happy-ever-after. I mean, look around…' She held her arms wide. 'This place is stunning; nature has painted a beautiful canvas of colour on the sky, everyone's happy and we're here to celebrate love. Of course there are happy endings.'

'I'm glad you think so. I just don't happen to share your conviction.'

'Why? Have you been hurt in the past?'

It was bold, but why not be bold? Life was too short to prevaricate, and time was running out to uncover what lay behind the cool, handsome mask that Dexter Stevens wore.

'No,' he said, obviously lying and turning away from the sea. 'Neither do I intend to be. I'm going back to the room.'

'To finish the all-important audit? To squirrel yourself away like Scrooge and pore over boring old facts and figures while everyone else is having a good time and there's this beautiful view to behold?' She braced herself, waiting for his response, her heart pounding.

He turned back round to face her and took a step closer, towering above her. The fresh, salty, warm summer evening air was eclipsed by the musky scent of him. Hands in his pockets, he looked into her eyes, studying her, that lock of dark hair falling forwards as he tilted his head.

'You want romance?' His voice was a whisper so soft that the sea breeze carried it away almost before she was sure she'd heard it.

Heart hammering, she looked up into dark blue eyes, glinting in the remaining light from the sleepy crimson-gold sun. He was looking at her as though he *knew* her and she could barely breathe as expectation pulsed between them.

'Who doesn't?'

'I don't,' he replied. 'But that isn't what I asked.'

'Of course I want romance.'

'I can't give you that, Tilly. I don't do relationships.'

She dropped her gaze, her heart slowing its pace, her breathing easing. Of course he didn't. So why was that such a devastating disappointment?

Dexter drew a hand out of his pocket and reached for her chin, lifting it gently between thumb and forefinger. She lifted her gaze, drawing in a breath as their eyes locked and everything around them faded into nothing. The intensity of his gaze drew her in with a power she hadn't known was possible.

'But I can give you this…'

He dipped his head and she held her breath as he brushed his lips against hers, sending a shocking wave of tingling, sparking desire right through her, making her stumble backwards. His hand went to her waist, steadying her. Instinctively, she reached up, placing her palms on his chest, her fingers spreading wide over his firm, sculpted contours. Holding her head gently with his other hand, he tilted her face upward, deepening the kiss, crushing her lips with his as she groaned beneath them. Sliding her hands up, rising onto tiptoes, she touched his neck and slid her fingers into his hair, pulling him in closer, only wanting more of him.

Then he pulled away. And she couldn't breathe for a long moment.

'I wouldn't call that romance,' she managed, conscious that her lips had cooled the moment he'd stopped kissing her.

'It's all I've got.' But there was still a fire in his eyes.

'I think you've got more than that, Dexter.'

The hint of a smile played at the corners of his mouth and his eyes flared with a golden glow. The atmosphere between them crackled and time stopped until he spoke, breaking the silence of their long gaze. He pointed across the castle courtyard.

'Shall we go back?'

For what? Was he offering his version of non-relationship romance in the bedroom? Was that what she wanted?

'The sun has almost gone now,' he continued. 'I don't want to leave you here on your own in the dark.'

Maybe he wasn't offering bedroom romance. He was being a gentleman. He might not be the archetypal romantic hero of a Hollywood movie, but Dexter Stevens was most definitely polite…and a gentleman. His morals didn't allow him to leave her alone out here in the dark.

'I'm going to watch the sun disappear first,' she replied, looking away and back out at the darkening sea, swallowing her disappointment.

'It's almost dark now. Come on, I can't leave you out here alone.'

It was enough to take her right back to the years she'd spent being protected from the world, when everyone around her had shielded her from what they saw as a danger, when she'd been frightened of everything. And it was enough to cause her well-practised heels to dig in. She'd fought hard to leave all that behind her. That was why Australia meant so much—it was her ticket to freedom. It was the way she was going to prove to herself and others that she was perfectly capable of taking care of herself. And, if she was going to take care of herself ten thousand miles away from home, she could certainly make the five hundred yards back to the castle.

'I'll be fine, thanks; I just want to watch the sunset.'

But only the topmost, orange crescent of the dying sun remained sitting on the horizon, waiting to slip beneath the waves.

'The sun has almost set,' he pointed out again. 'Come on; it's getting chilly.'

He was right. The temperature between them had gone from blazing heat to decided coolness and it

126 WEDDING FLING TO FOREVER

was because of him. The sun sank into the sea and was gone.

'I don't need looking after.' She walked towards him, but tripped on an uneven stone, and he caught her, steadying her.

'Of course not,' he replied. His lips were pressed together but the glint in his eyes told her he hadn't missed the irony. Chin tilted upwards, she marched past him as he stood watching her, before following and quickly catching up.

'Unless you're wearing high heels on uneven, thousand-year-old cobbles.'

'Apart from that.'

Damn him.

'Or get caught off-guard by a kiss.'

'That too.' She marched on towards the turret, her face burning, glad the cloak of darkness would hide her silly blushes.

'But not other than that?'

'Nope. So don't try to look out for me again, thank you.'

'Such belligerence. Where does that come from?'

Tilly pushed on the old wooden, studded turret door and it creaked open, but was so heavy she had to put her back into it and groaned a little with the effort. Dexter reached over her and pushed it open easily.

Damn him again.

She started up the spiral stone staircase.

'I guess it's a throwback to being locked away like Rapunzel when I was…' Her thoughts froze. *Where had that come from?* 'Younger.' She'd almost said 'ill', but she'd learned that lesson, hadn't she? And she didn't want Dexter doing a Lachlan and running a mile—not tonight.

'Rapunzel? What do you mean?'

She carried on up the staircase. 'Oh, nothing—my parents were a little over-protective, that's all. I feel a bit mean saying that, to be honest. They're lovely.'

'So you've wanted to prove your independence to your family.'

She glanced at him as she opened the door to the room. That was insightful, coming from a man who didn't seem to know that human emotion existed.

'Something like that.' She kicked off her sandals and padded over to the bed, picked up her bath robe and headed for the bathroom. 'Still do.'

'Hence Australia.'

'Exactly.'

Closing the door behind her, she stepped out of her dress and looked into the huge gilt-edged mirror. Her fingers went to the portacath scar— her reminder for ever of what she'd been through. Her reminder that its discovery by Lachlan—after months of trying to hide it from him and then trusting him enough to let him see it—had signalled the beginning of the end of their relationship. He'd asked about it, as she'd fully expected him to, and she'd been ready to explain. What she hadn't been prepared for was the horror on his face—the way he'd recoiled from it—or the way he'd distanced himself

128 WEDDING FLING TO FOREVER

until, a week later, he'd ended it. He hadn't wanted the responsibility, he'd said—he was too young.

Try actually having leukaemia, Lachlan.

Would she ever be free of her old foe reminding her it might still be there? That it could rear its head any time it liked and rob her of more time... or of life altogether? No, was the answer. The risk would always be there. Each year that had passed, she'd breathed a little more easily, until now, when she didn't think about it anywhere near as much. But she lived every day with the fallout.

Battling with people who wanted to protect her was one of its legacies. Wanting to be seen as normal, strong, capable, and starting over with a clean slate in a new job in a new place where no one knew of her past, was another. Counting her blessings, trying to take joy from every day, looking at the world with wonder and embracing all it had to offer were others.

Moving to London and taking her new job at Trafalgar Hospital was a test run—an attempt to try to start a new page before the much bigger goal that was Australia. She'd persuaded her parents that she'd be fine, that she was still close enough to home should she need them. But that had been more for their reassurance than hers...hadn't it?

She drew in a breath. She'd been fine. Yes, it had been a huge step moving to the city and yes, it was a little scary at times, but she was handling it. The confidence she'd missed out on building growing up was starting to build within her now. Every day, the city and her new role became more familiar and the urge to go running back to the safety of her warm, loving, secure home in the countryside became less. Being able to survive on her own on the other side of the world was slowly morphing from being nothing but a dream into reality.

She stared at her reflection and smiled tentatively—she was proud of herself for getting this far. The next step was the huge one, though, and her stomach flipped at the thought of it, but she tilted up her chin.

You can do it, girl. Go out there and live your life.

She leant in closer to the mirror and put her finger to her lips, running it along them.

Talking of living your life... They still looked the same but felt as though they ought to be swollen.

She'd taken what Dexter had offered. She'd embraced his kiss. Her heart began to pound a little harder and her breathing deepened. He'd said that was all he could offer, though. And he didn't do relationships, whatever that meant.

Pulling on the bath robe, she tied it at the waist.

Should she go out there and see what else he had to offer? Tingles shot down her spine, fizzing through her, heating her very core and thawing her objections to Dexter's gentlemanly protectiveness of her. She glanced back at the mirror. Her cheeks were pinker and she was biting her lower lip.

She wanted adventure, didn't she? Watching her reflection as her eyebrow rose and a slow smile spread across her face, she wrapped her arms around

130 WEDDING FLING TO FOREVER

herself, as though she was chilly. But it wasn't a cold chill that slowly spread through her; it was one of tingling anticipation. Life was way to short not to seize every possible opportunity there was and enjoy it.

She had a decision to make.

This was their last night.

He'd kissed her.

He wasn't offering a relationship or romance, but he did have more to offer than just a kiss.

Was that what she wanted?

She loosened the tie around her waist, pulling the fabric at her cleavage a little further apart...just enough to expose the hint of curves. She pushed her fingers up through her hair, licked her lips and opened the door to the bedroom.

If Dexter Stevens thought he had more to offer, she was sure as hell going to find out exactly what that was. Enigmatic, always composed, grumpy-bear Dexter had suddenly gone straight to the top of her adventure to-do list.

CHAPTER TEN

DEXTER SAT AT the desk, the glow from the laptop the only light in the darkened room.

'You're not going to work on that now, are you?'

'Got to be done,' he replied, not looking up.

Leaning against the desk, facing him, she glanced at the screen.

'That's not the audit.'

'I'm checking emails.'

'You're on holiday, for goodness' sake, Dexter; take a break.'

He looked up at her, his eyes flicking quickly from her cleavage to meet her own. But she'd seen him look and her pulse quickened.

'This isn't a holiday; it's a work event.'

'It's a wedding! How can that be work?'

'Because I'm *expected* to be here rather than *wanting* to be.'

'Oh, you complete killjoy!'

Dexter looked back to the laptop. 'Your name-calling vocabulary is far more extensive than I thought.'

Tilly folded her arms and sighed deeply. 'Do you prefer "curmudgeon"?'

'No.'

'"Grinch", then?'

He looked at her incredulously.

'I can see you trying to hide a smile now.' Tilly

dipped her head and leant in towards him, as though inspecting his face. 'I can see it; the corners of your mouth are trying to smile and you're fighting it. Let it smile…it won't hurt, I promise.' She grinned at him, taunting him playfully.

'Stop it.'

'Let it go, Dexter. That poor little smile is trying so hard to break through…and you're much more handsome when you smile.'

His eyes met hers and her breathing quickened. The same amber flames were in them that had been there on the battlements…right before he'd kissed her.

'Stop teasing me.' But his eyes weren't telling her to stop.

'I'm not the one doing the teasing tonight.'

'Which implies that I *am*?'

'You're the one who kissed me then pulled away and have acted as though nothing happened. I'd say that was pretty teasy.'

'Because you wanted more?' Dexter pushed back his chair and stretched his long legs out in front of him, folding his arms. A shiver ran down her spine, an awareness of her nakedness beneath the bathrobe rising within her. Having been emboldened by her need to feel alive, she suddenly faltered in the face of the intensity of his eyes and words. Suddenly, *he* was the one teasing *her*—the tables had been turned and he'd turned them.

She nodded slowly, not breaking eye contact.

Yes, she wanted more.

COLETTE COOPER 133

Dexter crossed an ankle over one knee and tilted his head to one side, observing her. 'Is that a yes?'

She held his gaze. What was she agreeing to? Another kiss? Or something more?

'I need to know.'

'You didn't stop to ask out there.' Tilly nodded towards the window through which shafts of silvery moonlight filtered through the old, mullioned glass.

'That was only a kiss,' he replied, sitting up straight and steepling his hands, his chin resting on his fingers.

'And what is it you're asking for my consent to?'

'I think you're looking for more than a kiss.'

'Only if you want more.'

Dexter stood and she drew in a breath as he took a step towards her, his warm, musky scent filling her nostrils, and she tilted her head upwards as he tilted his down. His lips were so near, the heat from them warmed her own, and it was all she could do not to reach a little higher to press her lips to his, to taste him.

'Only if you do, Tilly. I can't offer anything more.'

His breath was hot; it brushed her lips lightly, making them part. He was waiting for her to make the move this time. Was that what she wanted? Could she handle someone like him? Someone so sure of himself and in control? Someone so full of dark mystery? Someone who wasn't offering anything more than this night?

Life was short.

Pulling her phone from her pocket, she selected

a playlist and placed the device on the speaker on the desk. The soft, haunting, opening notes of 'Unchained Melody' filled the room.

'We missed the party tonight—you owe me a dance.' She opened her arms, holding them as though ready to waltz, watching him draw in a breath, his eyes not leaving hers. She took a step towards him, taking hold of his hand and placing it on her waist, then took hold of his other hand in hers, pulling him towards her gently until there was the merest breath of air between them.

'I don't know how to dance,' he murmured, his self-assurance disappearing, standing fixed to the spot, as though unable to move.

'Follow me.' She began to sway and after a moment felt him relax a little. Moving her feet, she took some small steps, swaying, turning a little, feeling the song build and Dexter relax more until he took over…and she realised he was leading her instead and had closed the breath of space between their bodies.

She hummed the lyrics about being hungry for touch, her eyes closed, lost in the song and the perfection of the moment. She looked up at him and he smiled down at her, gently…in a way she'd never seen before. His eyes left hers, focussing for a moment on her lips before gazing at her again, luring her in, robbing the breath from her lungs.

Life was short.

She lifted up onto her tiptoes, tilting her head as he dipped his, meeting his lips with her own, bringing her arms up and snaking them around his neck, pulling him towards her. Strong arms circled around her waist and drew her in impossibly closer, crushing her to him as he responded to her kiss, deepening it as they tasted each other, their tongues testing, probing and exploring.

But she wanted more. She found the buttons of his shirt, undoing them and pushing it from his shoulders, letting it fall to the floor. Her fingers were now able to explore the expanse of his broad, smooth chest and the firm contours of his well-defined muscles. But he took hold of her hands, stopping her, and for a moment she thought he was pulling away again, but his eyes told her something else entirely—their amber flames burned with aching desire and promise.

Yes, Dexter Stevens had much more to offer than a kiss. Holding onto her hand, he led her towards the bed in the centre of the room and stood in the shaft of moonlight that filtered in through the window.

'My turn,' he murmured, stroking her jawline with his finger before tracing it along her collarbone, over the curve of her breast and down between her cleavage to the tie that held together the only item of clothing she wore. He undid it, lowering his head to plant a featherlight kiss on the top of one shoulder as he slipped the robe from it, and then on the other shoulder, pushing the fabric until it fell to the floor.

Instinctively her hand went to her portacath scar but the silver moonlight that bathed them in a shimmering, gossamer-fine cloak was nowhere near bright enough to make it visible. Tilly watched him as he took her in. His eyes closed briefly as he took a breath, as if savouring the moment, before opening them again and fixing her with a gaze loaded with hunger.

'You're very beautiful,' he murmured, tracing his finger back along her collarbone, down through the centre of her cleavage to her navel and back up again. Every inch of her skin was on fire; every fibre in her being sparked as his hand trailed lower, cupping her breast. It sent a shockwave of searing heat through her as she arched her head back and he took the other breast in his other hand, brushing fingertips over hardened nipples, making her gasp and deepening her need for him.

Reaching for his belt, she tugged it, finding the buttons to his trousers, opening them and pushing them down until he could step out of them. Sitting down on the bed behind her, she looked up into his eyes. He remained where he was and she allowed her gaze to roam the length of his body, following the tantalising hollow down the centre of his perfect abs until she got to his boxers, just inches from her face, his erection straining against the fabric. She looked back up at him and he smiled slowly.

'I see now that you can offer much more than just a kiss, Dr Stevens.'

She raised an eyebrow and held his gaze as she slid backward onto the middle of the bed and lay on her side, one hand propping her head. She beckoned him, slowly as he placed one knee on the mattress, his eyes not leaving hers. Her pulse quickened, sending heated blood to every cell in her body and flaming her skin as he prowled towards her, his eyes never leaving hers. His body was perfection…and she wanted to feel it against her own; explore its dips and curves. He lay on his side, mirroring her, one hand supporting his head as he looked at her.

'Are you sure about this?' he asked. 'I've told you, I can't offer anything more.'

But, right now, this was all she wanted. This was enough.

She reached out and ran her fingers down his arm, reaching his fingers, lifting them to her lips and kissing them lightly before placing his hand on her breast, drawing in a breath as her skin flamed. His touch sent darts of desire zinging through her. But Dexter released her, moving away, and gut-wrenching frustration flooded through her. But he was smiling as he rolled off the bed.

'One moment,' he said, opening one of the drawers.

Ah… She'd have forgotten about that completely, but thankfully Dexter had retained at least a modicum of logical thinking. Striding back over to the bed and ripping open the packet, he rolled the condom on as she rolled onto her back, and in one swift movement Dexter was on top of her. Her thighs parted instinctively. All she wanted was to have him inside her—to quell the aching deep within her.

His eyes lingered on hers, burning, telling her he

wanted the same. And as he closed them he lowered down towards her and pressed his warm lips against her own, brushing her hardened nipples with his perfect chest. Pulses of desire surged through her as his erection nudged at the place between her thighs where she wanted him most. Instinctively, she arched towards him, groaning, breaking the contact between their lips, needing more air to feed her hungry lungs.

She opened her eyes to take him in. The soft moonlight glistened on his smooth skin and she placed her hands on his chest just to make sure he was real.

Was this happening? Was this perfect specimen of a man about to make love to her?

He wasn't the man she needed in her life long term—he wasn't safe, steady or reliable. But he *was* what she needed right now. Right now, she needed to feel alive, needed to take risks, needed to run free. Being given a second chance at life didn't mean simply doing more of the same. It didn't mean living a hum-drum existence. It didn't mean hiding away in corners, too scared to come out.

Dexter kissed his way down her throat as she arched her neck, taking his kisses on her collarbone and down on her breasts, sending darting flames down through her belly and into her core.

This wasn't doing more of the same. It was living, and she didn't have to try to relish every second, because every touch from his lips, his fingers and his palms set every fibre of her being alight.

It turned every atom within her into firecrackers that sparked, sending pulse after pulse of increasing, building pleasure coursing through her.

He brought his mouth back to meet hers, sucking at her bottom lip, pulling gently before easing back and looking deep into her eyes, increasing the pressure between her thighs and pushing forward as she parted them further. She gasped as he entered her then paused, closing his eyes, as if savouring the moment. Her fingers grasped his shoulders and he began to move, building the pace slowly. Her hips rose to meet him, his breathing more ragged as every rhythmic stroke built the tension further and further, until he brought her to the very edge of the exquisite precipice she knew he would take her crashing over. She held her breath for one long moment before he thrust into her again and sent her spiralling over the edge and freefalling into blissful, breathless oblivion. He arched, slowing the last few strokes, squeezing his eyes closed and groaning as he reached his own climax.

She wrapped her legs around him.

'Stay there,' she whispered, unable to bear the thought of him withdrawing. He rested above her on his forearms, breathless as she squeezed him with her thighs.

'I have to lie down,' he managed after a moment.

Reluctantly, she released him, and he lay beside her, his forearm on his forehead, eyes closed as his breathing settled.

Tilly looked up at the high stone-buttressed,

140 WEDDING FLING TO FOREVER

vaulted ceiling and then across at Dexter, almost jumping when met by his gaze. She smiled, shifting her position to lie on her side. He shifted too, smiling back—a smile rarely seen, which lifted his whole face and warmed her heart. How long they lay like that, she'd never know but, as her eyelids grew heavy and sleep settled over her, his eyes were the last thing she saw before sleep took her.

CHAPTER ELEVEN

LIFE HAD SUDDENLY got complicated.

How the hell had that happened?

Waking up, for a second he had not realised where he was. Then he'd turned to see Tilly sleeping beside him, her head to one side, her dark lashes fanning her cheeks with her ebony and amethyst hair spread over the pillow. He'd wanted nothing more than to watch her sleeping, wait for her to awaken and make love to her all over again.

He'd also wanted to run. Because it had become more than obvious that his feelings for her were much more than physical. It wasn't only the two days they'd spent at the castle, when they'd worked so well together on Geetha's grandpa or when he'd found himself wanting to tell her a little about his past. It wasn't only that her presence had meant that he'd actually enjoyed parts of the wedding or that she'd coaxed him into running barefoot in the sand and dancing to a slushy love song. No, this had been happening for longer than that. Tilly Clover had been affecting him for months.

'Thanks for listening, everyone.' The sales rep's voice broke into his thoughts. 'Any questions?'

Yes. What on earth made me think that sleeping with Tilly would result in anything other than trouble?

He'd been straight with her. He'd told her he didn't

do relationships. But it wasn't her he'd needed to explain that to…it was himself. And he'd promptly forgotten his own words.

They'd spent almost every minute together at the wedding. They'd been back for two days.

And he missed her.

It had been his choice to get up the morning after they'd slept together and go for a run along the beach before she'd woken up. When he'd got back to the hotel, she'd been down at breakfast with some of the other guests. He'd told her he didn't do relationships and she'd taken him at his word, clearly treating their night together as a classic one-night stand.

It was his usual MO. Except Tilly wasn't like any other woman he'd ever spent a night with. And he wanted more of her. But the rules of the game had been set and they were both obeying them.

He'd got what he wanted.

No promises.

No commitment.

No emotion.

But he did *feel*. He felt things he'd never felt before and it scared the hell out of him. That was exactly why he'd bottled it that morning.

Dexter got up, walking towards the door and slipping in his wireless earbuds—his way of preventing people from speaking to him. He could get back to the department. Back to Tilly—his one-night stand.

It was what he'd wanted…wasn't it? No strings?

But it didn't feel right. He was unsettled, uneasy, edgy…as if he'd made a mistake but wasn't

COLETTE COOPER   143

quite sure what it was he'd done wrong. Maybe he shouldn't have slept with her. Maybe he shouldn't have placed restrictions on it.

Pushing open the doors to the department, Dexter saw Mark.

'Everything okay?' he asked the charge nurse.

'Well, I'm not going to say the "Q word", but it's under control at the moment. The parents have arrived, by the way.'

'Parents?' Not saying the word 'quiet' was one of those silly unwritten hospital rules designed not to tempt fate, which Dexter thought was ridiculous superstition.

'Of the two lads in from the RTC earlier? They'd like to speak to you.'

'Oh, yes. Where's Sister Clover?'

He needed Tilly. It was his now instinctive reaction. He was only too aware of his own limitations when it came to speaking to relatives. He didn't have any problem explaining the clinical situation, but relatives always wanted much more than that. And he knew that was where he fell short. Tilly had become his go-to person when it came to handling situations like this.

But that had been before they'd slept together… before he'd broken his own rules and allowed himself to feel something for her. Her revelation about Australia had shocked him but it was probably best she was going, so he could take back control and stop spending every minute of every day thinking

144   WEDDING FLING TO FOREVER

about her. It was the logical solution to this problem he'd brought on himself.

'Right here,' she said, walking towards them. And inexplicably he relaxed, his heart lighter. Her pretty, floral scent filled his nostrils; her light, musical voice lifted him.

This was the very definition of illogical.

'We need to go and speak to the parents of the two boys from the road-traffic collision.'

'Okay,' she replied. 'No problem. Mark's already had a tray of tea sent in.'

Dexter nodded, staring at her. Staring at the woman who, against his better judgment, had muddied his thoughts, made him question what he wanted and wonder if he'd maybe even begun to have feelings for her. She'd made him smile; she'd made him want to dance and actually feel the music in his soul; she'd made him want to wake up with her in the morning, make love to her all over again and slake his hunger for her.

But, as much as he'd wanted those things then, the realisation that he wanted them again had troubled him ever since. It meant he wanted her more than he'd ever wanted anyone. Which meant he cared. And he didn't want to care, because caring weakened a person. It left them vulnerable…wide open to whatever the person they cared about wanted to put them through.

Anyway, he'd never be enough for her. Tilly wanted romance—he didn't even believe in it. She lived to have fun—he was so uptight, he hadn't even been able to relax enough to feel comfortable at a wedding party.

'Shall we?' said Tilly, her palm outstretched towards the door.

Dexter hesitated. He needed to clear the air. This was the first shift they'd worked together since the morning after their huge mistake. The morning after the night they'd made love. The morning he'd slid out of bed quietly, like a thief in the night, and had pounded the beach until he could run no more instead of facing her and what she'd made him feel.

He opened the door to a laundry cupboard near the relatives' room.

'We need to talk first,' he said, indicating she go inside. He followed her in, closing the door. They stood opposite each other beside the racks of freshly laundered white linen.

'Something wrong?' she asked.

He took a breath. 'We have to work together, Tilly, in spite of…what happened at the wedding.'

She smiled. 'Don't worry; I won't tell anyone you had a dance.'

He raked his hand through his hair. 'Can you be serious, just for once?'

Her smile disappeared and he instantly regretted the sharpness of his tone.

'What happened shouldn't have happened, Tilly. I wish I could turn the clock back and make it unhappen, but I can't, and we have to work together, so we just need to…' He paused for breath. 'We just need to forget it ever happened.'

146 WEDDING FLING TO FOREVER

Tilly took a step back into the shelving laden with white sheets, her complexion fading almost to match their colour. She blinked, staring at him.

'Wow.'

He frowned.

'Okay, Dexter... I understand. I didn't really need the explanation, given you'd already set the rules with the whole "I don't do romance or relationships" thing, but thanks for making sure I'm fully in the picture. Appreciated. Shall we go and see these parents together—professionally?'

He nodded, opening the door, relieved to have got that conversation over with. At least they'd be able to work together without there being any awkwardness between them now. They both knew where they stood. His position was clear and his life was back in order. But that uncomfortable edginess still niggled at him.

They went into to the relatives' room, in which sat two sets of highly anxious parents waiting to speak to him to find out about the car crash their sons had been involved in and to ask the question he always dreaded: *Are they going to be okay?*

He didn't know the answer. And he never knew how to respond when they shed tears or wanted to hug him. He preferred it when they got angry. Anger, he could deal with. He'd honed that skill many years ago as a small child.

'Get me a kebab from the chippy,' his father would yell, waking him in the early hours, reeking of beer and cigarettes.

'I don't have any money, Dad,' he'd reply quietly, inching to the top corner of the bed against the wall, as far away from his father's reach as he could get.

'I gave you some the other day. What have you done with it?'

'That was last week, Dad… I bought your cigarettes with most of that and a couple of pies for tea the other night.'

'Don't cheek me… Go and get me a kebab or you'll feel my belt on your backside.'

And Dexter had dressed quickly and walked down to the kebab shop with the few pennies he'd tried to save in the hope of buying some food for lunch at school the next day. Emre, the kebab shop owner, had often let him off paying full price, but he'd known he couldn't rely on the man's kindness too often.

Anger was best managed by being numb to it, by avoiding it at all if possible, and if it couldn't be avoided then meeting it with passive acceptance. It was how he'd got through his childhood. Being numb meant not feeling pain.

'You're very welcome to stay here,' said Tilly, leaning forward and lightly touching the hand of one of the mothers opposite, who was tearful. 'Or I can take you up to ITU so you'll be there when they arrive on the unit from Theatre.'

The meeting with the shocked parents went well. Tilly was her usual warm, empathic, supportive self, handing out tissues along with kind, well-chosen words. They didn't weep, didn't need a hug and weren't angry.

He wasn't transported back to a time when fear for his own safety had been paramount in his mind and he'd had to hide his own feelings of terror at what his father did to him. He'd hidden those feelings so well for so long that he no longer knew if he could express them at all... In fact, if he could express any feelings at all any more. His father's violent rages, his unwillingness to care about anyone but himself, his mockery of everything Dexter ever did and, worst of all, the repeated accusations that he'd been responsible for the death of his mother had been the most effective anaesthetic against feeling pain...against *feeling*.

But one question lingered in Dexter's mind. He'd mastered the dark art of denying emotion, of pushing it away and refusing to acknowledge it, but there remained a fear that he'd inherited the traits of his father.

What if a drink turned him into the same man? What if he allowed emotion into his life and let go of the tight self-control he'd wound around himself? What if he cared about someone—what would happen then?

He'd learned to deal with other people's anger but it was the uncontrollable anger that he might have within himself that terrified him the most. The uncontainable fury his father had unleashed time and time again, even when he'd lost his job, had all but destroyed their home and had made a frightened enemy of his only son.

What if he'd inherited that? He didn't want to find out. He didn't want to become his father.

Which was why keeping feelings out of his life, all feelings, was his only option. If only he'd remembered that when he'd allowed Tilly into his life. If he had, maybe his well-ordered world wouldn't be shaking on its foundations right now.

The cardiac-arrest alarm suddenly sounded, shrill and very loud, and Tilly leapt from her seat, walking swiftly towards the red flashing light over cubicle two, wheeling the arrest trolley as she went, then throwing back the curtain.

'Anaphylaxis,' said Dexter. 'Eight years old; came in with severe abdo pain and pyrexia. Penicillin given; no previously known allergies.'

Tilly drew up the required drugs as Dexter took a plastic airway from Anika and inserted it, attaching oxygen and giving two squeezes on the reservoir bag he'd attached to it. He instructed Pearl to take over airway management as he reached for defibrillator pads, ripped the backing off them and applied them to the child's chest. The green waveform showed them what they suspected: a flat line.

'Compressions,' said Dexter, looking at Tilly directly, but she'd already kicked the footstool into position and stood on it, hands poised above the child's chest.

150 WEDDING FLING TO FOREVER

'What are you doing?' shrieked the child's mother who'd got up from her seat and stood next to Dexter.

'IV adrenaline,' said Dexter. 'Please sit down, Mrs Green, I need space to treat your daughter.' Flipping back the top of the cannula, he pushed the drug into the child's vein.

'What's that?' said the mother. 'What are you giving her? Doctor, you need to save her—she's my only child.'

'I'm doing my best, Mrs Green; please, just give me a little space.'

'Anika, can you take over compressions please?' asked Tilly, moving aside to let her in.

'Let's stand here,' she said to the distressed mum, taking her by the shoulders and moving her gently to the edge of the cubicle to keep her away from Dexter as he tried to save her daughter's life. 'Lottie's had an allergic reaction and the doctor is giving her a medicine that we hope will reverse that. The oxygen is to help her breathing; the other doctor is helping her heart to beat until the medicine begins to work.'

'IV fluids,' said Dexter. 'Crystalloid; ten mil per kilo, stat. Check rhythm.'

They all stopped what they were doing.

'Sinus bradycardia,' he announced. 'Stop compressions; adrenaline.' He administered more of the drug.

'Her heart's beating again but is a little slow,' explained Tilly. 'So we're giving a little more of the medicine to bring it back to a normal rate.'

'Is she…going to be okay?' asked the little girl's mum, clutching Tilly's arm.

'Spontaneous breaths,' called Pearl as the little girl gave a cough.

'Remove the airway,' ordered Dexter. 'Heart rate sixty-five; BP rising. Hello, Lottie, are you waking up?'

The little girl's eyes flickered open; she looked puzzled.

'Lottie!' shrieked her mother, letting go of Tilly's arm. 'Don't ever do that to me again.'

'My throat hurts,' said Lottie.

'You can have a little drink in a moment,' said Tilly, relief flooding through her.

'Thank you, Doctor,' said Mrs Green, flinging her arms around Dexter's shoulders and holding him, vice-like, as he stiffened until she released him.

'You're welcome,' he replied, taking a step backward the moment he was released, straightening his dislodged stethoscope and running his hand through his locks of hair that had fallen forward.

He met Tilly's gaze briefly before looking down and away.

'Good work,' he said, addressing the team. 'Pearl, can you prescribe an antihistamine and a non-penicillin-based antibiotic?'

'Sure,' replied the registrar.

'Anika, can you clear up for me, please?' said Tilly. 'I'll write the notes up. Mrs Green, I'll speak to you again before you go up to the ward.'

'Thank you, Sister.'

152 WEDDING FLING TO FOREVER

'Fairly straightforward,' said Dexter as they made their way to the nurse's station.

'It was very straightforward as far as paediatric cardiac arrests go,' agreed Tilly. 'Right up until the point it was all over.'

'What do you mean?' said Dexter, pulling out a chair and sitting down in front of a computer.

'Until the grateful mum hugged you and you turned into an ironing board.' She looked at him, a dark eyebrow raised.

'I don't do hugs.'

Tilly glanced around but no one was nearby. 'You do sometimes,' she whispered. 'But don't worry; I won't tell anyone about that either.'

Dexter drew in a breath, seemingly engrossed in the screen in front of him.

Tilly glanced around again, her voice still low. 'What happened doesn't need to affect our working relationship. We both knew what we were doing.'

She hadn't expected him to have left by the time she woke up that following morning, but really, he'd been clear about his stance—he didn't do relationships. What should she have expected? And he'd reinforced his feelings on the matter very clearly, earlier in the linen cupboard, leaving her in no doubt at all about how he felt. She wasn't going to allow herself to be hurt just because he'd preferred to go for an early-morning run along the beach than wake up with her, or that he was so desperate to make sure she knew that the offer of his version of romance had been a limited, time-only deal.

He nodded, still staring at the screen, apparently engrossed in a page of blood results. 'Good.'

'Still a man of few words.' Nothing had changed. They'd spent two days together. She'd thought they'd made some sort of connection. He'd opened up a little but he'd closed right back down again. And she only had herself to blame. She'd known months ago that she shouldn't go anywhere near Dexter Stevens. But she'd ignored that huge red flag warning her to keep away from him.

She'd wanted adventure. And she'd got it. And now she had to live with the fallout: stinging rejection; mulling over where she'd gone wrong. Had he felt the portacath scar? Unlike Lachlan, Dexter would have known straight away what it was. But, like Lachlan, perhaps he'd not wanted the responsibility either.

Whatever. He wanted a professional-only relationship and she could do that. She refused to be hurt. She refused to let it show at least.

'Lactate,' he growled.

'Beg your pardon?' said Tilly.

He pointed to the screen. 'Bloody lactate. How many times do I need to tell them? Doing a lactate is part of the sepsis screening.'

Tilly stared at him. She'd never heard him swear before or appear irritated. Cool and standoffish, yes, but not outwardly irritated.

'Well, just ask someone to do it now.'

'It should have already been done.' He sighed and jabbed at the keyboard, closing it down. 'I've got an

154   WEDDING FLING TO FOREVER

exec board meeting and, as the department doesn't need me right now, I have no excuse to get out of it.'

He stood, scraping back his chair, and walked away from her, stopping only to speak briefly to one of the doctors, no doubt to instruct them to do a lactate on the patient he'd mentioned.

'No, now!' were his parting words to a slightly startled Pearl.

Whatever had got into him? He usually kept his feelings on a leash more taut than a tightrope.

'Tilly, I've got a six-year-old asthmatic in Paeds; would you give me a hand with him? Mum's pretty anxious and not really helping…' It was Ally, one of the other junior doctors.

'Of course,' said Tilly, following her, and frowning as the door Dexter had just gone through banged shut.

CHAPTER TWELVE

TILLY GLANCED AT the clock on the wall. *How had it got to four o'clock already?* She'd made sure the other staff took a break, but had yet to take one herself, and was by now desperately in need of a coffee and something to eat.

Sitting at the nurse's station, she sensed Dexter approach. Was it his too-familiar warm scent she'd noticed or his dark shadow approaching and falling on her? Her stomach knotted. A large hand appeared in her line of vision and placed a lidded cardboard cup in front of her on the desk. She looked up… into piercing cobalt eyes…and her stomach knotted further.

'Peace offering,' he said, lips pressed together, watching her.

She frowned, looking from him to the cup and back again. 'For what?'

'For being what you would no doubt call a "sourpuss" earlier.'

'A sourpuss?'

Dexter sighed. 'Or Scrooge, or maybe a killjoy… or, dare I say it, a party pooper?'

A slow smile spread across her face. It was good to have the banter back. Maybe having a professional-only relationship with Dexter would be okay.

'Slightly uptight grumpy bear,' she said, noting

156 WEDDING FLING TO FOREVER

the quiver at the corners of his lips. He raised a dark eyebrow and nodded slowly.

'I'll give you that,' he replied, his lips curving very slightly towards what could have turned into a smile had he not looked away. 'Drink that.' He nodded at the cardboard cup. 'We can't have you keeling over.'

'Thanks,' said Tilly, picking it up. 'Is it coffee?'

'Strong and black, just as you like it… It's what you ordered at breakfast…at the wedding.'

He'd remembered how she took her coffee…

'You looked like you needed it,' he added.

She rolled her eyes. 'Extra shifts. The money's great but they do take their toll. My flat looks like I abandoned it months ago and, although I love my job, I'd quite like to see walls that aren't A&E walls some time.'

'Thanks for everything, Sister, Doctor.' A grateful patient was wheeled past the nurse's station on his way to a ward.

'You're welcome,' replied Tilly. 'Don't be in a rush to visit us again.'

The patient smiled. 'I won't.'

'Another happy customer,' said Tilly, smiling at Dexter.

He raised an eyebrow. 'Leaving only forty-three patients in the department still to be seen.' He held up his hands. 'And, before you say it, I'm well aware that's a very *Grinchy* comment to make.'

'It certainly is, Dr Stevens. What astounding self-awareness you have.' She took a sip of coffee.

'Developed possibly because, almost continually for the last four months, you've been pointing out to me that I have a slightly more serious side than some.'

Tilly snorted, suppressing a laugh and bringing her hand to her mouth. 'Don't! You nearly made me choke.' She placed her cup back down on the desk.

'Did I say something amusing?' The trace of a frown appeared between his brows.

She pressed her lips together, trying not to laugh, then shook her head. 'I give up, Dexter. I've tried, but you are who are, and I'm just going to have to accept that.'

His frown deepened. 'What's that supposed to mean?'

Go for it, Tilly. You've nothing to lose.

'I'd always wondered if you had hidden depths lurking beneath your cool demeanour... Maybe a sense of humour; perhaps an ability to open up a little, or possibly to show some emotion, some passion.' She bit her lip. 'And you do...sometimes.' She picked up the cup of coffee and took a drink, watching him from over the rim.

His frown melted as he looked at her and his dark eyebrows rose. Then he smiled...slowly. A devastating smile spreading outwards and lighting up his eyes, giving them a rare sparkle that squeezed all the air from her lungs.

'Careful; someone might see you,' said Tilly, still eyeing him from the rim of the cup.

158 WEDDING FLING TO FOREVER

He leant in closer, his voice low. 'That's your fault.'

'My fault?' She feigned innocence and held onto the cup as though it protected her from his sudden nearness and the intensity of his gaze, which was doing untold damage to her heart rate. A gaze she'd thought she would never see again.

He gave an almost imperceptible nod. His eyes were mesmerising, inches from her own, his soft breath whispering across her face as he spoke. He glanced away for a second as a porter walked past the nurse's station and she immediately missed being held in his gaze. But his eyes locked back on her before her heart rate had time to adjust back to normal.

'You do that to me, Tilly.'

Every nerve ending in her entire body became alert.

He glanced around but there was no one nearby. Their hard work today meant that the department was currently under control.

'I make you smile, you mean?' Her pulse raced.

'Smile, laugh, dance, run headlong into the sea fully clothed...'

'But not want to be romantic?' she challenged.

His eyes held hers, searching them, as if trying to decide what to say or do next. 'Come with me.' He stood, tucking his chair under the desk.

She looked up at him. 'To where?'

'We have a meeting.'

'We do?'

Ally walked towards the desk. 'Dr Stevens, can I

COLETTE COOPER 159

just ask you about taking a day's annual leave next Wednesday?'

'Yes,' he replied. 'It's fine. Send me an email for the leave booking system.'

Ally looked taken aback. 'Oh, wow…great, thanks.'

'Sister, we have a meeting.'

Tilly picked up her coffee, got up and followed him to her office. He held open the door and closed it behind them, turning the lock with a click. Heart hammering, she stared at him. Somehow his eyes had darkened.

'What's the meeting about?' she asked, clutching her cup, a flush of warmth spreading through her.

'Romance,' he replied, walking towards her, taking the cup from her hand and placing it on the desk behind her.

She swallowed. 'Romance?'

'The word keeps cropping up…it must be important to you.'

He was inches away from her; she could feel his warmth, inhale his scent.

'It's important to most people.'

He smiled, his eyes locked on hers, smouldering embers igniting within them. Tingles shivered down her spine.

'I have a sense we've been here before, Tilly.'

'You told me you don't do romance.'

'I don't.'

'Or relationships.'

'No…but I *do* do this.'

Dipping his head, he closed his eyes as his lips

160   WEDDING FLING TO FOREVER

brushed hers, their bodies remaining chastely, tantalisingly, apart. But she wanted more than a chaste kiss. Dexter Stevens didn't do romance, but he knew how to kiss, and she knew only too well that he had more than this to offer. She closed the gap between them, reaching up and drawing him towards her, pressing against his warm, hard body and hearing his groan as she raked her fingers into his hair. She gasped as he pulled her closer, deepening the kiss, tasting her and leaving her in no doubt that he wanted her.

She didn't want to pull away but she needed air, and pulled back, breathless, her heart racing. Dexter's pager sounded and he groaned.

'Timing.' He unclipped the pager from the waistband of his scrubs, glancing at it. 'I'll have to get this.'

'Of course,' she managed, pulling her uniform straight.

'Would you like to go to dinner this evening?'

'Okay…'

Dinner? But he regretted them sleeping together, didn't he?

'Seven p.m. at the Italian on Queen's Walk, by Tower Bridge?'

She nodded. 'Sounds good.'

He lifted his mobile phone, tapping to find his contact, unlocked the door and was gone.

She couldn't move.

What had happened?

She sat down on the edge of her desk, unsure if

her legs could take her weight any more. The heat that had cooled so quickly between them since the castle, and had been doused further a short time ago in the linen cupboard, had flared into life...out of nowhere.

Unless it hadn't been from nowhere.

Had he changed his mind?

What if he wanted more than a one-night stand?

What if he wanted to break his own rules?

She glanced at the clock. The shift was over. It was just as well, because there was no way she could think straight now, and if she was going to negotiate a new set of rules with Dexter she really needed to be able to think.

CHAPTER THIRTEEN

DEXTER ARRIVED AT the restaurant early, making sure they had the best table, overlooking the River Thames from the south bank. He checked his watch, glancing up when the door opened, then reached for his glass of orange juice and took a long drink. But his mouth was still dry.

Why was he so nervous?

He looked out of the window. A pleasure cruiser sailed by, disappearing under the bridge. People walked past, pushing prams, walking dogs. A grey squirrel ran up a nearby tree. Normal, everyday activities were going on all around him but nothing felt normal or every day.

How long had he managed to keep his distance from Tilly after the castle? Two days off work and then half a day once he'd seen her again. He'd tried not to think about her all the time. He'd tried not to miss her. He'd tried really hard not to want to smile when she walked into the room, and he'd tried even harder not to remember how it had felt to have her in his arms and make love to her.

But he'd failed…epically…and he was very aware that he'd become a little irritable as a result. He'd apologised to Pearl for his outburst earlier.

He hadn't planned to ask Tilly to dinner, just as he hadn't planned to take her into the office on false pretences and kiss her. But he'd seen that playful, sexy flare in her eyes over that coffee cup as she'd caught his look… His resolve had evaporated and the words had tumbled out of his mouth.

But he didn't do relationships. Or feelings.

Leaning back in his seat, he raked his fingers through his hair. He was being tested. Could he hang on to what he believed in—that logic was the best policy and feelings, emotions, were for the weak? Clearly not, because he was sitting here in this restaurant waiting to have dinner with the only woman who'd ever made him question that belief.

He spotted Tilly in the distance and his heart rate immediately quickened. Tilly, with her beautiful amethyst eyes, infectious smile and irrepressible love of life—the woman who'd made him smile and laugh when he'd thought they were things everyone else did. Who'd made him want to tell her about his past and made him question every truth he knew about himself.

Was he really someone who didn't know how to have fun?

Was he the cool-hearted killjoy she'd accused him of being?

She had a point. In fact, she'd probably read him perfectly. Being like that kept people away from him. It stopped him from having to deal with feelings, emotions and everything that came with those uncontrollable human faults: the rejection, pain and fear.

It hadn't kept her away, though, had it? And he'd found himself wanting to be with her, spend time with her and get to know her. Gradually, without him even noticing until it was too late, she'd percolated into his being, making him want to smile, laugh and do things...illogical things...he'd never done before.

Perhaps his logic was flawed.

And, though he'd tried to shake the thought from his mind, he'd even begun to wonder whether the reason his resolve had weakened and he'd kissed her again earlier was because he'd begun to develop feelings for her. He'd looked into her eyes and seen them flame and it had sent a shot of desire through him. But it was more than sexual chemistry that had filled his senses these last few months.

'So sorry I'm late,' said Tilly, sitting down in the chair he'd pulled out from the table for her. 'I fell asleep when I got home. Thanks.'

'You fell asleep? It was a pretty busy one today but I didn't think it was that bad.'

'It was on top of an evening shift I'd done the night before,' she replied, reaching for the menu. 'Cumulative effect. Have you chosen yet?'

'I'm going to have the *arrabiata*.'

'I think I'll join you. Shall we share a garlic flatbread?'

'Sounds good.'

She picked up the wine list automatically, but then remembered. The waiter took their order and she asked for a sparkling water.

'Don't let me stop you from having a glass of wine,' said Dexter.

She grimaced. 'It'd probably put me to sleep again. I'll stick with water.'

The waiter came over and they put in their order.

'You think my company will be enough to put you asleep? Charmed, I'm sure.'

But he was smiling that rare, warm, genuine smile that made his eyes sparkle and made her want to gaze into them. There was no way Dexter's company would put her to sleep, especially after that kiss earlier. She'd been annoyed she'd fallen asleep when she'd got home after work—she'd wanted more time to get ready. As it was, she'd only had time for a quick shower, a change of clothes, a whisk of mascara and a slick of lip balm. And now, with his eyes on her, she wished she'd had time to do more.

'I've never been bored in your company, Dexter... not even for a second. You're very entertaining.'

He looked at her quizzically.

'Entertaining? Dare I ask how?'

She pressed her lips together, her eyes narrowed thoughtfully, her chin resting in one hand.

'In many ways.' She lifted an eyebrow.

'Name one.'

'Ooh, let me see. You're an excellent teasee.'

'I don't think that's actually a word.'

'Oh, it is—it means someone who's good at being teased.'

'And I'm good at that?'

'Most definitely. You're so straitlaced.'

'Not always.'

He gazed into her eyes across the table, through the flickering flame of the candle, and her breathing quickened. There had been nothing straitlaced about how he'd lured her to a 'meeting' in her office and kissed the breath out of her. Or about how he'd taken the lead from her as they'd danced at the castle and moved her towards the bed. Or about how he'd made love to her. And there was nothing straitlaced about the fire in his eyes right now.

'No, not always.'

The waiter brought the food and she reluctantly dragged her gaze from Dexter's to acknowledge him. She didn't want to break the spell between them. She wanted to reach over and touch his lips; she wanted everyone else to disappear and leave them alone together. And, from the way he was looking at her, it seemed he wanted the exact same thing. The black ink in which he'd written into his rule book his self-imposed rules of the game was fading to grey.

Tilly glanced out of the window and across the river to the Tower of London.

'We seem to be drawn to castles.'

'But we have a river this time, and not the sea, so my trousers might survive the evening.'

Tilly laughed.

'The night is young—anything could happen.'

He looked at her over the flickering candlelight, the glow from the flame taking her back to the sunset on the battery terrace…right before he'd kissed her. Would he kiss her again tonight? Her pulse quickened. She wasn't going to stop him if he did.

They turned to their meal.

'Any dessert this evening?' asked the waiter shortly afterwards, collecting their plates.

Yes. I'll have the man sitting opposite.

'Not for me, thanks,' replied Tilly, raising a questioning eyebrow at Dexter.

'Me neither…we need to get back. Just the bill, please.'

The waiter nodded and took the dishes away.

'Need to get back?' repeated Tilly, a smile playing on her lips. 'Do we?'

Her heart rate picked up as she saw unmistakeable desire flame in his eyes.

'You're tired.'

'Am I?'

'You fell asleep earlier.'

'I'm not tired now.'

He swallowed, his Adam's apple sliding in his throat. 'We have work tomorrow.'

Tilly checked the time on her phone.

'I'm allowed to stay up after nine p.m.…even if I have work the next day.'

He looked at her as though he was trying to work something out.

Was he deciding if he wanted more than a one-night stand? If he wanted to finish what he'd started in her office?

They paid the bill and stepped outside. Grey

168 WEDDING FLING TO FOREVER

clouds had slipped in front of the sun and the air had cooled.

'I'll get a cab,' said Dexter, looking up at the sky. 'Looks like rain.'

'I fancy a walk along the river…come on.'

They walked along the riverside path of Queen's Walk, past Tower Bridge and a family of ducks, watching a couple in a canoe paddle past.

'It's so peaceful here,' said Tilly. 'A little out of the city centre… Makes a nice change.'

'I bring the dogs out along here sometimes for a walk.'

'I still can't get over how you love your dogs.'

'Why is that so hard to believe?'

'I don't know.' Her lips pressed together in thought. 'I'd always thought of you as…'

'An unemotional, antisocial Grinch?'

She feigned a look of being impressed.

'Again, such self-awareness.'

He rolled his eyes. 'I just thought I'd save you saying it.'

'Actually, that isn't what I was going to say. What you told me at the wedding about your father puts it into context…makes how you are much more understandable. Did you ever have counselling?'

Dexter looked at her quizzically. 'I don't need counselling.'

'You went through a huge trauma growing up… losing your mum, too. If ever you need to talk about any of it, I'm quite a good listener.'

'I don't…thank you.'

COLETTE COOPER 169

A clap of distant thunder sounded.

'Sounds ominous,' she said, looking up at the sky.

'We should have got that cab,' replied Dexter. 'I can feel rain.'

'Oh, we'll be fine…a drop of rain never hurt anyone. Anyway, I like being in the rain. It's refreshing, and a good storm always makes you feel so alive, doesn't it? Come on, let's walk.'

Another clap of thunder.

'It's getting closer,' said Dexter.

'Walk and talk quickly, then. Now we've cleared the air from the awkward morning after, we can relax with each other a bit, can't we?'

Dexter looked doubtful.

'Dexter, look, we had sex—it happens. And, hey, it's the twenty-first century—you don't have to worry, I'm not expecting you to marry me. Chill out.'

He stared at her, his eyes wide, and she laughed.

'I had a boyfriend once who was the exact opposite of you.' She continued walking along the river path.

'So I'm not even your type, then,' he replied, falling into step with her.

'Far from it, Dexter, so you really needn't worry—I'm not looking for a happy-ever-after from you.'

'So who was this person?'

'Lachlan. He was a guitarist in a band I met on a night out from work.'

'And in what way was he the exact opposite of me, dare I ask?'

Tilly smiled. 'He was—probably still is—a very "rock 'n' roll" sort of guy. He liked a good time, loads of fun…always looking for the next adventure.'

'Sounds perfect for you. But it didn't last?'

'No,' she replied. 'And that's where the differences between you end. Lachlan, much the same as yourself, didn't want commitment.'

He didn't want the commitment of being with someone who might need to lean on him a little one day.

'And you were looking for commitment?'

It was a little more complicated than that, but she wasn't going to tell him about her illness. He'd literally run away after spending only one night together. She could imagine how far and how quickly he'd run if she told him she'd had cancer and that it could come back at any time.

'Sort of,' she replied. She looked up at the sky. The clouds were darker. A large rain drop landed on her upturned face and she held out her palms.

'It's definitely raining.'

'We're not too far from the next bridge,' said Dexter, turning up the collar on his jacket. 'We can shelter under there.'

'Your turn, then,' said Tilly. 'What about your romantic past?'

'I don't have one.'

'Oh, no, of course. You don't do romance. Tell me about your last girlfriend, then.'

'Helena.'

'Don't do that to me, Dexter—don't go all mysterious one-word answers on me now. What happened?'

'She taught me that happy-ever-afters don't exist.'

Thunder crashed overhead so loudly, it made Tilly duck. And then the heavens opened.

Dexter drew his jacket more tightly around him but Tilly stood, face upturned, arms spread wide as another clap of thunder crashed and the rain came down heavier, soaking her in seconds.

'Come on,' said Dexter, raising his voice over the noise of the falling rain. 'Don't just stand there; we need to get under cover.'

'No,' called Tilly, laughing. 'This is your chance to prove it.'

'Prove what?' he replied, pulling up his collar further.

'That you're not Grinch.' She twirled round on the spot, face still turned up to the sky, her eyes closed. 'Walk in the rain with me. Let yourself get soaked. Don't run from it…embrace it.' She opened her eyes to look at him. He stood with his shoulders hunched, his dark hair getting darker by the second. 'Come on, Dexter, live a little.'

'I'd hoped to stay dry this evening.'

She grinned at him. 'It's too late for that.'

A puddle had formed on the path in front of them. Tilly stood on the edge of it and jumped in, both feet together, the water splashing up her legs and making her laugh. She turned to face him, her hands on her hips.

'Do it,' she ordered, pointing at the puddle.

Dexter shook his head slowly. 'Not a chance.'

'Don't be a—'

She didn't have chance to complete her sentence. Dexter jumped into the puddle and stood before her, trying to suppress a triumphant grin. Tilly gave him an approving smile then turned, ran over to one of the old black Victorian-style lampposts, hooked her arm and swung around it, belting out the old Gene Kelly track 'Singin' in the Rain'. She stopped and beckoned him.

'Absolutely not,' he shouted back as more thunder crashed overhead. 'That's where I draw the line.'

Tilly laughed and ran over to him, grabbing him by the hand.

'Come on,' she said. 'Run in the rain with me.' She pulled his hand, breaking into a run, and they ran along the river path, through puddles and back towards the city until, breathless and laughing, they reached the sanctuary of Tower Bridge.

Tilly leant against the wall, pushing her soaking hair away from her face and getting her breath back. Dexter had his hands on his knees but recovered quickly. He looked up at her and, although her breathing had been settling, suddenly she was breathless all over again…but for an entirely different reason.

Their eyes locked and he took a step towards her.

'You keep doing this to me,' he said, searching her eyes, as though trying to work out how she'd done it.

'Doing what?'

'Getting me wet, making me run with you…making me want to kiss you.'

Her heart thudded so hard, she feared it might stop.

'Not on purpose.'

He raised an eyebrow.

'I think you know full well what you do to me, Tilly.'

'But you don't do romance.'

He shook his head. 'No.'

'And yet, in the right circumstances, holding hands and running through the rain can be extremely romantic.'

'Can it?'

She nodded. 'As can being kissed under a bridge.'

A slow smile curved his lips. 'Is that what you want?'

She held his gaze. 'I think that might be nice. What about you?'

His eyes flamed. 'I think it would be more than nice, Tilly.'

He closed the space between them, placed one hand either side of her head on the wall of the bridge behind her, enclosing her, and brought his lips to hers. She closed her eyes, inhaled his warm scent and tasted him, running her fingers up into his drenched hair.

This *was* romantic.

He could be romantic.

And she wanted more.

'I think my place is closer,' she managed as he

174 WEDDING FLING TO FOREVER

pulled back. 'If you'd like to…' *Come and take your wet clothes off* '…dry off. It sounds as though the rain's easing.'

He swallowed, searching her eyes again before nodding and holding her gaze.

'I think I should…dry off, yes.'

CHAPTER FOURTEEN

LEAVING TILLY IN bed to get home and changed before returning to the hospital for his shift had been monumentally hard. He hadn't gone to dinner expecting it to end with them sleeping together but it had quickly become apparent that that was where the evening was going. The chemistry between them was undeniable, and Tilly inviting him in had left him in no doubt that sex was on the agenda. How they'd kept their hands off each other until they'd got inside the flat, he didn't know. But this time, unlike at the castle, he hadn't sloped out at dawn, regretting what had happened—far from it. It had been a wrench leaving her.

The Saturday evening chaos in the department at Trafalgar began a little earlier than usual with the arrival of a small group of men who'd been to a football match and begun drinking too much, too early and had various injuries as a result of some sort of fracas. There'd been no need for him to intervene other than to brief the Plastics team on the details of the wounds.

'Dr Stevens?' said Tilly. 'Would you have a look at a patient in four? I think she's dislocated her shoulder.'

'Sure,' he replied.

Tilly lowered her voice. 'The poor woman is six months pregnant and says she fell down a step. I'm

176 WEDDING FLING TO FOREVER

not sure I believe her but we can investigate that after her shoulder has been dealt with. I've tried to assess her but I think she'll need a muscle relaxant before we can examine her. I've immobilised it in a sling for now.'

'What do you mean, you don't believe her?'

'She's got an old bruise under her right eye that she's tried to cover with make-up and, when I asked her about it, she said she'd stumbled and hit a kitchen cupboard.'

'I suppose she might have,' said Dexter. 'Pregnancy can affect balance due to the hormone relaxin, which increases in order to relax the uterus and pelvic ligaments. It's quite common for women to fall when pregnant.'

'There's something not quite right, though,' said Tilly. 'She's jumpy and nervous, like she doesn't want to be here. We should assess her fully and maintain a high level of suspicion she may be vulnerable.'

'Let's go and see her,' said Dexter. 'And we can take it from there. We'll take a muscle relaxant in with us.'

'Hi, Becky,' said Tilly, entering the cubicle. 'This is Dr Stevens, one of the consultants. Is it okay if we have a look at that shoulder?'

'Of course,' said Becky, clearly in pain and holding her arm very still. 'I could do with getting home, really.'

Tilly glanced at Dexter. Becky wanting to get

home quickly was one of the warning signs she'd told him about. People who were being abused were often wary of the authorities.

'I'm just going to remove this sling so the doctor can examine you, Becky. Hold your arm nice and still for me.'

Becky grimaced as Tilly removed the sling and pulled down the gown to expose both shoulders, being careful to minimise the exposure to maintain Becky's privacy and dignity.

Dexter moved to stand at the bottom of the trolley. 'I'm just going to look first, Becky,' he said.

Tilly watched him as he studied Becky's shoulders, looking for any asymmetry. She'd already made a mental note of the faded bruises to their patient's chest.

'Just going to palpate the shoulder now,' said Dexter, moving from the end of the trolley and standing at Becky's shoulder.

'The doctor's going to feel the shoulder, Becky,' explained Tilly, throwing Dexter a look that hopefully reminded him to drop the medical jargon.

'Is it going to hurt?' said Becky, her eyes wide.

'Hard to tell until we try,' said Dexter. 'But, if it does, we'll stop immediately. I want to check your elbow and wrist joints, too.' He palpated the wrist and elbow before placing his hands on the shoulder. Although Becky winced as he moved his fingers over the joint, she wasn't in too much pain. 'The humeral head is palpable anteriorly—no need for an X-ray. There's no evidence of neurovascular

178   WEDDING FLING TO FOREVER

compromise. We'll do a closed reduction, but let's get some muscle relaxant in first.'

Tilly raised an eyebrow at him. He narrowed his eyes then seemed to understand.

He addressed Becky. 'I can feel that the top of the humerus…the arm bone here…' he touched Becky's arm '…has popped out of place. That's why it's so painful when you move it. It's very fixable, though. We simply need to pop it back into the socket. With this injury, there's also the possibility of nerve and blood vessel damage, but I've checked, and you don't have that. So, if you're happy, we can do a reduction—'

Tilly coughed.

'We can manipulate…move…the arm bone back into place,' he continued. 'We'll give you something for the pain first, though.'

'Have you got any questions, Becky? Was the doctor's explanation okay?' said Tilly. 'And is there anyone I can call for you, to sit with you and take you home afterwards?'

'No,' said Becky. 'There's my husband, but I don't…' She glanced at Tilly and then at Dexter. 'He's at work.'

'Injection going in,' said Dexter. 'We'll give that a few minutes to work and then come back.'

Tilly made sure Becky had the nurse call-bell to hand, instructing her to call if she needed anything, then she joined Dexter in the clinical room. 'What do you think?' she asked him.

'She has multiple contusions, all at varying stages

of healing, on the face, chest and upper back,' said Dexter, rubbing the back of his neck. 'Her wrist was tender when I examined her for neurovascular compromise and there were old, finger-sized bruises on it.'

'And she wants to get home,' added Tilly, her lips pressed together. 'And she didn't want me to call her husband.'

'Looks as though you're right. She needs referring to the safeguarding team. We have a duty of care to her. It would be good to get her consent but, if we can't, we still have to make the call and raise the concern. Do you want to try to talk to her after the procedure?'

She nodded. 'I'll see if she's willing to give me any information but invariably people are reluctant for fear of reprisals. It's so frustrating.'

'In a way, it's quite fortunate she's come in with only a dislocated shoulder,' said Dexter. 'It could have been far worse, and at least now we can help her.'

Tilly looked at him. He wasn't simply a one-dimensional, unfeeling, cool operator all the time, was he?

'What?' he said, stepping back, searching her eyes.

Tilly smiled. 'Nothing. Shall we go and sort Becky's shoulder out?'

Tilly was well aware of the personal safety measures every member of hospital staff needed to keep in

180 WEDDING FLING TO FOREVER

mind at all times. The problem was that, when she'd initially entered the cubicle to speak to her after she and Dexter had successfully repositioned her dislocated shoulder and applied a sling, Becky had been the only person in the cubicle.

But that had just changed. And the situation escalated very quickly. They were joined by her more than slightly irate husband, Chris, who had called her when he'd found she wasn't at home. And, rather than having come directly from work, he appeared to have travelled via the pub.

'She says she's fine,' he said through gritted teeth. 'So she's coming home.'

Tilly drew in a breath, her exit from the cubicle now blocked by the man, willing her heart to slow a little and her voice not to rise an octave or two.

'I just need to monitor her a little longer. An injury like this can cause nerve and blood vessel damage. You're very welcome to go and get a cup of tea from the café, or I can call you later if you prefer.'

'I'll stay here,' he growled.

'Go and get a drink,' she replied. 'I'm sure you could do with one after a long day at work.'

It was the typical behaviour of an abuser—they didn't want their partner to interact with the authorities for fear of being outed. And the conversation Tilly had already had with Becky, along with the physical evidence, convinced her that this ruddy-faced brute standing before her now was an abuser.

'Have you called social services?' he demanded, taking a step closer towards her.

She stood her ground, not wanting to appear afraid of him and give him the upper hand, but her pulse was racing, her mouth was dry and every muscle in her body was rigid. She was in full fight or flight mode. Becky had refused to be referred, saying it would only make things worse. She lifted her chin, controlling her breathing.

Challenge him.

'Why would I have done that?'

'Because you lot like interfering.' He took another step closer, jabbing a finger towards her. The smell of alcohol and cigarettes intensified, turning her stomach. The need to step backwards and away from him was overwhelming but there was nowhere to go.

'Leave her, Chris,' said Becky. 'She's just doing her job. I haven't told her anything.'

The man swung round to face her, grabbing the metal sides of the trolley on which she was sitting, putting his face up close against hers and spitting words like venom.

'I haven't told her anything,' he mocked. 'Brilliant, Becky, brilliant; that's just made nosey nurse here think we do have something to hide…nice one.'

'I'm sure nobody meant for any of this to happen,' said Tilly.

He swung back to face Tilly, rounding on her, the stench of his breath cloying and hanging heavily in the air between them. She stepped back, bumping into the bedside locker, knocking a glass of water to the floor with a crash.

182 WEDDING FLING TO FOREVER

'Are you accusing me of hitting her?' He bore down on her, his eyes bloodshot, his voice overly calm but sounding a warning.

She swallowed. 'We all have difficult times in our relationships. There's help available if you're struggling.'

'You *are* accusing me of hitting her.' He bore down towards her again, so close now that his face was slightly out of focus. He clamped his hands, one either side of her on the bedside locker behind her, trapping her and pinning her to it. She bent backwards, instinctively trying to create even a little distance between them, but his body was pressed so hard against her that she couldn't move.

The cubicle curtain parted behind him and Tilly's eyes darted to it.

Dexter!

The man followed Tilly's gaze, turning to face him, releasing her from his grip.

Dexter stood, his expression one of mild interest but his stance firm, legs apart, arms by his sides. He was all carefully controlled restraint, appearing almost disinterested, but his hands were balled into tight fists and his knuckles were deathly white.

'Everything all right in here, Sister? I heard a crash.'

CHAPTER FIFTEEN

THE RAISED VOICES had made Dexter look up from the computer at the nurse's station; the smashing of a glass that followed had caused him to leap from his seat, stride over to the cubicle and drag the curtain aside. Ice gripped him, freezing him, locking the air in his lungs in an instant as he took in the scene.

The instinctive reaction to lunge at the man and rip him away from Tilly shocked him, and forcing himself not to took every atom of self-control he possessed. He'd been in similar situations before in A&E but he'd never, ever, had the overwhelming urge to strike someone before. Every sinew in his body was taut, every muscle rigid; his fingernails dug into his palms. But that would be wrong; it would be counterproductive and could escalate the situation, putting Tilly in danger.

Instead, he did what he always did: wore his mask and appeared calm, controlled and unemotional. The only difference was that this time, in this particular situation, he didn't feel those things. He couldn't take the emotion out of it.

A well-built, brutish-looking man with an unshaven, weather-beaten face turned round and looked at him, swaying slightly. He was drunk. And Dexter was transported straight back to when his father's angry face and swaying body had stood before him as a child.

184 WEDDING FLING TO FOREVER

He clenched his fists more tightly and tried to control his breathing. Aggression, he could deal with—he did it almost every day to one degree or another—but aggression due to drunkenness triggered something deep inside him, especially when there was a child involved. And this child, the one Becky was carrying, was so very vulnerable.

'I'm just checking Becky's shoulder,' said Tilly, clearly trying but not quite managing to keep her voice light.

'There's a coffee shop out by the main entrance,' said Dexter, addressing the man. 'Sister will be half an hour—just long enough for you to have a hot drink before you come back.'

The man curled his lip into a snarl and walked towards him, making him tense further, every muscle straining and ready to act if he had to. If the man did strike out, he would be left with no alternative but to physically restrain him.

'If anyone else tells me to go and get a drink, I swear to God I'll—' There was the stench of cigarettes and beer… It was his father all over again.

'Or I can have you removed from the department,' Dexter cut in. 'Your choice.'

The man narrowed his eyes murderously and the two men watched each other for an extended moment. Dexter's expression remained impassive, belying the shocking, raging turmoil beneath.

Make the right decision. Don't make me have to contain you.

Because I will. Because I'm not letting you go anywhere near Tilly again.

Because...

'Do your checks, but I'll be back in fifteen minutes and *she's* coming home.'

The man walked out of the cubicle, past Dexter, being careful not to brush against him, just as Security turned up.

'Everything all right, Doc?' asked Simon, the guard.

Dexter nodded and turned to Tilly.

'I'll get someone else to take over here.'

'I'm fine,' she replied. 'I just need to speak with Becky a moment longer.'

He didn't want to leave her. He wanted to take her into his arms. But Tilly, typically, was putting her patient first.

He turned to the security guard. 'Stay here—he'll be coming back in ten minutes or so.'

'You'll put me out of a job, Doc,' said Simon, grinning and turning to Tilly. 'And he does it with much more class than I do, doesn't he?'

'He does.' Tilly gave him a smile but not her usual wide, warm smile. She'd clearly been frightened. He desperately wanted to hold her but it wasn't possible right then.

Instead, he walked to the changing room a little further down the corridor, his pulse still racing. There was no one else in there and he stood in front of a long mirror on the wall, leaning towards it and

186 WEDDING FLING TO FOREVER

resting his forehead on the cool glass as his breathing slowed.

What had happened out there?

He straightened up and looked at his reflection. *Finish your sentence, Stevens. You're not going to let that brute anywhere near Tilly again because...?*

He looked into cool blue eyes. *Because you want to protect her. Be honest. Because you're in love with her.*

He swallowed. *Was he?* Was that why he'd felt so angry? Was that why he'd wanted to take hold of the man and tear him off her...*because he was in love with her?*

His refection frowned at him. It all sounded so logical. His reaction had been instinctive because he *cared.* It made sense. But what was terrifying was the anger he'd felt because she'd been in danger— an anger he'd never experienced before. Was that because he'd never cared so deeply before?

If he did care for her, it had crept up on him with impunity, without him giving his permission.

How the hell had that happened?

And if he did care for her...love her, even...just look where it had got him. It had unleashed the very thing he'd tried so hard to keep under control all his life: anger. Boiling, raging anger that had made him want to lash out at someone.

So he had *inherited his father's propensity for rage.*

In the right circumstances, he was capable of letting feelings get the better of him. Years of practice at not caring, putting on the mask and not succumbing to emotions—gone in a flash because he'd allowed himself to care.

And now he had to try even harder to control it. That meant not caring. And definitely not falling in love.

He went to the sink, washed his hands and splashed cold water onto his face, wiping it dry with a paper towel. He strode back towards the department. Becky's husband would be back soon and he had to get to her before the man returned and took her home. He wasn't going to allow another child to grow up with an angry, aggressive, alcoholic father and have no support, and he wasn't going to risk that child growing up without its mother either.

Simon stood outside the cubicle.

'Anyone in there?' said Dexter.

'Just the patient and Tilly,' he replied.

'Can I come in?' he called through the curtain.

Tilly pulled open the curtain. He closed it behind him, glancing at Tilly with a questioning stare. She shook her head.

'Becky doesn't want to be referred.'

Damn it.

He stood beside her, resting his hands on the metal side of the trolley, looking down at them. This was hard. Give him a multiple category-one trauma any day rather than have to deal with this side of the job. But it had to be done. He wasn't going to accept that there was nothing he could do for this mother and her baby.

'I know you're frightened, Becky,' he began, lifting his eyes to look at her. 'And I know you think that one day Chris might change…might become the husband and father you want him to be.'

'He will,' she insisted. 'Once the baby is born, he'll change. He just gets so angry, but it's not him—it's the drink.'

Dexter had heard it all before. The same words had been in his own head as a child every time his father had lashed out at him. Every single time that belt had slammed into the backs of his legs he'd convinced himself it would be the last time, that his father would change…be the father he wanted him to be. It had never happened.

But he and his father had never had what he was able to offer Becky. 'He's not going to change, Becky. Men like him never do, not without help and lots of support. If you want you and your baby to stay with your husband and both be safe, you're all going to need support. There is help out there to get him off the drink and there's support for you and the baby.'

'He won't want social services involved.' She looked up at him with frightened, wide eyes.

'He doesn't need to know. I'm going to refer you to the physiotherapy service,' said Dexter. 'They happen to be in the same building as the safeguarding team here at the hospital. I'll explain to your husband that you're going to need appointments for a long time for that shoulder injury.'

She looked into his eyes and he saw the exact moment that the penny dropped.

'Yes,' she said. 'The appointments will be in the day time, won't they?'

'They will,' replied Dexter. 'When your husband's at work. And there's help available with transport, too, if you need it.'

Becky reached for his hand. 'Thank you, Doctor; thank you so much.'

'I'll make the first appointment and the number for the centre will be on the card...if you need to contact them in the meantime.'

Becky nodded, biting her lip.

'I'll explain about the physio to your husband when he gets back.'

'Thank you.' She released his hand.

'Let's get you ready to go home, Becky,' said Tilly. 'While Dr Stevens sorts out your referral.'

'You okay?' said Tilly, sitting down beside Dexter at the nurse's station later. Becky and her husband had gone home. Dexter had walked down to the café to find Chris and tell him his wife was ready, and they'd walked back together, Chris in a much more agreeable disposition.

'Fine,' he replied, tapping the keyboard, updating Becky's notes.

'Can we have a meeting?'

He glanced across at her.

'When? What for?'

WEDDING FLING TO FOREVER

Tilly nodded at his screen. 'When you've finished that. My office.'

'I'm done,' he said, logging off. 'Is there a problem?'

'Come on then,' she replied, standing.

Dexter got up and they walked the short distance to Tilly's office. She closed the door behind them, and he remembered the last time they'd both been in this room together...when he'd locked the door and kissed her.

'Have you brought me in here to seduce me again, Sister?'

She smiled. 'My recollection is that it was you who seduced me, Doctor.'

He stroked his chin thoughtfully. 'So it was. So, why have you called this cosy meeting? Have I done something wrong?'

'I just wanted to check you're okay after what happened with Becky and her husband.'

He folded his arms. 'I'm fine. Is that all?'

Tilly leant against the desk. 'You were thinking of your father.'

'I rarely think of him.' He uncrossed his arms, digging his hands into the pockets of his scrubs.

'You thought of him just then. That man reminded you of him. That's why you were so angry and why you went out of your way to help Becky.'

How did she know this? He glanced round behind him at the door then looked back at her before dropping his gaze. 'I'd have helped her anyway.'

'Your actions this evening have given that baby

a better start in life than you had, Dexter. You were brilliant.'

'I just hope they're okay.' When he'd gone down to the café to find Becky's husband, he gave him a chance to do the right thing. He'd given him the number for a counsellor. He'd not blamed him; he'd told him he understood how hard it was to stop drinking; that he didn't need to be the way he was; and he'd explained that he could have a better, happier life...be a role model for his child.

'They have a much better chance of being okay now than they ever had before.'

He looked up and met her gaze. There was no pity in her eyes...just approval. Like the approval he'd always hoped he'd earn from his father one day; like the approval he'd known he'd have had from his mother...if she'd lived.

How could he stop himself from falling in love with Tilly?

It was already too late for that.

CHAPTER SIXTEEN

'MAJOR INCIDENT DECLARED,' said Tilly. 'Serious fire in an office block in the city; all emergency services in attendance and we're the first receiving hospital for any casualties—let's get beds in Resus and Majors freed up and prepped. Pass this on to colleagues, please. Let's go.'

'You okay?' said Dexter. Tilly updated the electronic board as discharged patients left the department to create space for any of the fire's casualties.

'Could do without this, to be honest,' she replied. 'I've had an extra coffee this morning and still can't wake up.'

'First casualty inbound,' called Ally. 'ETA eight minutes. Adult male with smoke inhalation, currently conscious and responding.'

'Resus, please,' said Dexter. 'Early intubation if warranted.'

Tilly rubbed the back of her neck and opened her eyes wide, trying to wake herself up fully.

What was wrong with her today?

It wasn't just today, though, was it? She'd been increasingly tired for a while now—she'd even fallen asleep the other night instead of getting ready for dinner with Dexter and had had to turn up only half-ready. She closed her eyes, snapping them open again quickly. Was the tiredness due to something more than the extra shifts she'd been doing?

Her haematologist's words rang in her head.

Don't ignore any symptoms, Tilly.

The doors to Resus crashed open and two paramedics wheeled in their first patient.

No time to think about that now.

'Ciaran O'Connor, thirty-five, on the fourth floor of the office block where it appears the fire started; extricated by the fire service; no external burns; conscious and breathing; tachypnoeic and sats of eighty-nine on ten litres of oxygen.'

'Thank you,' said Dexter. 'Can you manage to shuffle over onto the trolley, Ciaran?'

Tilly stood on the other side of the trolley, guiding him over. The poor guy was indeed tachypnoeic—his breathing rate was way beyond normal. 'Well done; we're going to be checking you over and taking a blood test from your wrist to measure your oxygen levels, okay? Any questions?'

Ciaran shook his head, coughing.

'I'm just going to remove this mask to have a look at your airways,' added Dexter, lifting the oxygen mask from the patient's face. 'Soot in the mouth and septum. Just going to listen to your chest.' He slid his stethoscope from around his neck and bent, listening. 'Bilateral wheeze. Salbutamol nebuliser, please, Sister; I'll do the ABG.'

Tilly dealt with the nebuliser as Dexter took some blood for an arterial blood gas.

'I'll run that through the gas analyser,' she said, holding out her hand. He handed it to her and she took it to the small room next to Resus, slotting the

194   WEDDING FLING TO FOREVER

syringe into the sampling port in the machine and clicking the 'analyse' button.

As she waited, her hand went to her portacath scar, her fingers running over the raised bump. She should have her bloods checked.

The analyser beeped and whirred as it printed out the results and she tore the paper, glancing at the figures as she walked back to Resus and handed it over to Dexter.

'Respiratory acidosis,' he said, glancing at it. 'I've organised a bronchoscopy before he goes to ITU. Ally, can you take a resus back pack and do the transfer, please?'

Ally and Mark left Resus with Ciaran just as patient number two from the fire came through the doors—a thirty-three-year-old, again with smoke inhalation. Tilly greeted the woman with a reassuring smile and began the process again.

By the time the incident was over, there had been twelve patients from the fire, all with varying degrees of respiratory compromise. The major incident had been stood down but there were still other patients to be seen.

She needed to think. *Should she make an appointment to get her bloods done? Could she ignore this any longer? She really didn't feel great.*

'Are you okay?' said Dexter, approaching her at the patient board as she stood assessing the situation in the department. 'You've not been your usual self today. I haven't heard you singing even once.'

'It's been busy.'

'It's always busy—and you always sing, or hum, or just generally sparkle. Is something wrong?'

'I don't have to be the life and soul all the time.' She hadn't meant to sound so sharp but she felt awful. She just wanted this shift to end and get home to sleep...and wake up, feel fine and not have leukaemia. She couldn't go through all that again.

Please don't let this be happening.

He held up his hands. 'Sorry.'

'Sorry, Dexter, I've... I've just got something on my mind, that's all.' She wasn't going to tell him what. The last time she'd talked about it to a man, he'd disappeared from her life at warp speed. She wasn't making that mistake again.

'Do you want to talk about it?'

'No.' Absolutely not. Dexter was the last person she wanted to tell. The king of no emotion? He wouldn't understand how she felt.

A slight frown flitted across his brow but was gone in a flash, his mask intact again.

'Okay, if you're sure.'

She managed a tight smile, but a wave of nausea hit her like an express train and suddenly her legs wouldn't hold her weight. She remembered reaching out, remembered strong arms catching her and then everything went black.

Distant voices...calm and urgent at the same time.

'Blood pressure?'

'Ninety over forty,' came the reply.

Too low.

196 WEDDING FLING TO FOREVER

'Heart rate?'

'Ninety-seven.'

Too high.

'Pass me a cannulation tray and blood bottles.'

Dexter?

'Sharp scratch, Tilly.'

It *was* Dexter.

Slowly, she opened her eyes, looking round sleepily.

'And she's back in the room,' said Mark. 'Welcome back, Tilly.'

'You fainted,' said Dexter, ripping the backing off the cannula dressing and smoothing it in place. 'Your blood pressure and heart rate are returning to normal but I want you to stay lying down.' He turned to Mark. 'Can you get these to the lab asap, please?'

Mark took the samples from him. 'Don't do that to us again, Tilly—it creates way too much paperwork.' He grinned and left the cubicle.

'Perhaps you should cut back on those overtime shifts after all,' said Dexter, pressing the button on the monitor to check Tilly's blood pressure again. The machine whirred as it inflated the cuff around her arm.

'Maybe,' she replied, glancing at the monitor as the cuff deflated. The reading was better. 'Can I sit up a little now?'

'A little.' Dexter raised the head of the trolley so that she was semi-reclined. 'I'd say you definitely need to cut back your hours. Covering shifts to help out is all very laudable, but not at the expense of your health, Tilly.'

'It's not the shifts.' The extra shifts weren't to blame, were they? She knew the signs to look out for. She'd been warned the leukaemia might come back. She'd been increasingly tired for a few weeks now. And there was no point in trying to hide it any longer. Dexter had taken bloods and the results would be back in the next couple of hours. He'd know instantly what was wrong with her.

'You've been doing too many, and too close together, without enough of a break in between. Just cut down a little.'

'It's not the extra shifts, Dexter.'

She was going to have to tell him. Lachlan's face swam into view in her mind. The horror on it when she'd finally told him about her illness… The way he'd moved just slightly, away from her… The way he'd dropped his gaze, unable to look at her when she'd gone further and said that there was a chance she could relapse…

Not telling Lachlan at first hadn't really been planned. He'd been her first, what she'd thought, serious boyfriend and they'd just been having so much fun—going to gigs and hanging out with his band and other bands on the circuit. It had been a whirl of new experiences, new people. The leukaemia had been forgotten. She'd thought they were in love. She'd thought he cared and that she could trust and rely on him—maybe that he'd stand by her.

She'd been wrong.

198 WEDDING FLING TO FOREVER

She and Dexter weren't in love. He didn't do romance or relationships and didn't believe in happy-ever-afters. And, even if she'd held a secret hope that he might make an exception for her, what she was about to tell him would put a very clear line under that ever happening.

'You haven't been eating and drinking properly, either, I suppose—that won't have helped. You need to look after yourself more, Tilly.' He leaned in towards her over the silver rail of the side of the trolley, his hand moving towards hers. But he stopped, glancing behind him at the cubicle curtain, withdrawing his hand, quickly. 'I'll cook for you this evening…make sure you get a good meal inside you.'

She squeezed her eyes shut and a heaviness fell over her. Dexter was a good man. She didn't want to lose him…didn't want him to run, as Lachlan had. But she had to tell him the truth. She couldn't let him sit in front of a computer to check her blood results and find out about her illness that way. The king of no emotion wasn't emotionless at all, was he?

She took a breath. She'd survived before and she would do again…even if the process was painful.

Be positive, Tilly.

'You can cook?' She smiled at him.

'Don't look so surprised.' He feigned indignance with a dramatically turned-down mouth. 'I do a mean lasagne.'

'Is that what's on the menu tonight, then?'

'If that's what you want.'

COLETTE COOPER

199

'Sounds great,' she replied.

'And cookie-dough ice cream to follow?'

'It's like you've read my mind.'

They held each other's gaze for a long moment. What passed between them, she wasn't sure, but suddenly she knew she not only *had* to tell him about the leukaemia—she *wanted* to.

'Can you clip the "Do Not Enter" sign to the curtain, Dexter, please?'

He did as she instructed, returning to stand beside her.

'What is it?' he asked, his eyes dark, serious.

'I had acute lymphoblastic leukaemia as a teen. You might find that my blood results show a relapse.' She searched his face. He wore his mask. 'I just wanted to warn you before you saw the results.'

She saw his Adam's apple slide in his throat and his lips part, just a little.

React, Dexter. Say something. Show something... even if it's horror. She held her breath. Was he going to run?

'I didn't know.'

'No reason you would. When I started at Trafalgar, I told HR I didn't want anyone to know.'

'Why?'

'Because when people know you've had cancer, they treat you differently...they treat you like you're made of fine china. I didn't want to be a patient any more. I just wanted to be like everyone else, you know? Normal.'

'I see.'

WEDDING FLING TO FOREVER

She looked up into concerned blue eyes and found she couldn't hold it back any longer.

'Every time they started the syringe driver and the chemo began to drip... In my head, I went to Bondi beach; I walked along the shore and watched the surfers dipping and cresting; I actually felt the warmth of the sun on my skin and the softness of the sand. I even dreamt up what the hospital I'd work in looked like—I had no clue then, of course, but I could build the picture in my mind and even imagine treating patients...making them better.'

'That's where the Australian dream began?'

She managed a small smile. 'A nurse got me to imagine myself somewhere nice. I chose a beach and she guided me through experiencing the beach with all my senses...you know the sort of thing... touching the sand, hearing the waves, tasting the salty sea air...'

'And it helped?'

'It gave me hope. I went back to that beach so often over the years. After a time, the imagery developed from simply feeling the sand between my fingers to imagining the beach house I'd live in; the beach sports I'd take part in. Then I began the research—looking up where I could go to make it all a reality some day. Dreaming and planning made it seem real, even though I knew it might never actually happen... So real, I began to believe it could happen. I got so close...'

'It could still happen.'

'Maybe my family were right—maybe I over-estimated myself; dreamt too big. Maybe I can't look after myself as well as I thought I could. I've been naive.'

'No. Tilly, you're one of the most capable people I've ever met—of course you can look after yourself. And you definitely didn't dream too big; it's a wonderful dream to have. Come on, don't pre-empt the results; they could be fine. Where's that sparkle I…?'

She glanced up at him. *Why had he faltered?*

'Know so well?' he continued.

'It's taking a break. Normal service will…*may*… be resumed at some point.' *With any luck.* Dexter was right—she wasn't handling this in the right way. What had happened to her? Her usually instinctive positivity had deserted her and turned her into a Grinch. She smiled at her choice of word and the irony of it. There was she, being exactly what she'd accused Dexter of being.

She glanced up again, hoping to reassure him that she was still herself, but his deep blue eyes were still full of earnest concern, which he was usually so good at concealing.

'Oh, I'm fine, really.' But the tears came from nowhere, filling her eyes, stinging as she tried to smile through them. 'Look at me! Ignore me, I'm being silly.' She sniffed and fished in her pocket for a tissue.

'Hey, hey, come on; it could all be fine.'

'It's just such bad timing,' she managed, her breath hitching. 'I need to reply to the agency in

Sydney to accept the start date. What am I supposed to say to them? They'll give the job to someone else and...' She blew her nose. 'Sorry, it's just... I wanted this so much.'

'And there's still a good chance you can have it. Wait for the blood results—you can't do anything until you have those. Do you need a hug?'

She looked up into intense, kind blue eyes.

Dexter Stevens was offering a sympathetic hug. He wasn't high-tailing it out of there.

She nodded and he wrapped her in his arms as she sank into his chest.

'You've never said that to me before.'

'I've never said it to anyone before.' He kissed the top of her head, making her smile. She dabbed at her nose again, sniffing and smiling at the same time. 'I'm honoured.'

'I'll cook dinner for six thirty. Is that okay?'

'Six thirty is fine,' she replied.

'Good. I'll pick some cookie dough up from the supermarket on the way home.'

'But what about the blood results?'

'What is it we always say, Tilly? Never jump to conclusions...wait for the results. But, whatever the results show, I'm introducing you to the culinary delight that is my home-made lasagne this evening. If that's okay with you?'

She smiled. It was more than okay. It was exactly what she needed. All she had to do now was wait for the lab to send the results to Dexter. What happened after that entirely depended upon them.

CHAPTER SEVENTEEN

'DR STEVENS?'

Dexter looked up from the X-ray he'd been reviewing. It was Mark.

'Can you cast your eyes over this X-ray?' he asked, handing him a tablet that showed the black-and-white image of a child's skull.

Dexter took the tablet from him. 'What am I looking for?'

'It's of a six-year-old who fell through a broken fence in the garden,' explained Mark. 'He has a laceration to the right occipital area, which I can close with glue, as long as you think there are no fragments of fence in the tissues.'

Dexter scrutinised the image carefully. 'No fragments; you can go ahead with glue. Don't forget an anti-tetanus if he hasn't had one.' He handed the tablet back to the charge nurse.

'Sure, thank you,' said Mark.

Dexter returned his attention to the X-ray on the screen in front of him but became aware of Tilly's voice not far away. He looked up. She was talking to a woman who carried a toddler on her hip, stroking the child's head and smiling.

What the hell was she doing?

He got up and went over to them.

'Anything I can help with, Sister?'

'We're all good,' she replied. 'Dylan here man-

204 WEDDING FLING TO FOREVER

aged to get his hand stuck in his toy truck this afternoon, but we've got it out now, haven't we, Dylan?'

The little boy nodded and his mother shook her head. 'Kids,' she said, rolling her eyes. 'You've gotta love 'em! Thank you, Nurse.'

Tilly laughed. 'You're very welcome. You're good to go now. No harm done. Bye, Dylan.'

Dylan waved behind him as his mum carried him out.

Love. That word kept popping up. He'd almost said it to her, hadn't he, when he'd mentioned her lack of sparkle...the sparkle he *loved* so much? But he'd stopped himself from saying it and changed the words.

'He was cute,' said Tilly, giving a last wave as Dylan and his mum went through the doors.

Dexter stared at her. 'What *do* you think you're doing?'

Tilly stared back. 'My job.'

Dexter lifted his arm, swishing his hand in a circle. 'Back to the cubicle.'

'I'm fine.'

'You're a patient.'

'Not any more. There's someone else in the cubicle.'

'What?'

'I didn't need it; I'm okay. I'm just waiting for results, that's all.'

Dexter put his hands on his hips. 'Unbelievable.'

'Thank you.' She grinned at him.

He shook his head. 'And completely obstinate.

I can't have you wandering the department, Tilly, you're officially a patient until I discharge you.'

'Discharge me, then.'

'Not yet. You'll have to go somewhere else, then.'

'Where?'

'Your office? The café? Anywhere but here.'

'But I'd rather be busy.'

Dexter got that. It made sense. It was logical. 'Do me a favour,' he said.

'Does it involve sitting on a hospital trolley worrying for the next hour or so?'

He wished he could take the wait away…wished he could make her results normal.

'I've written up a further report with recommendations on Becky Johnson for the safeguarding team. Would you go through it for me—check it reads okay and see if you think I can add anything else to make it stronger?'

She nodded approvingly. 'I can do that. I'll be in my office.'

He watched her walk away and go into the office before he was satisfied she wasn't going to take a detour and go and see another patient. Her results wouldn't take much longer. What if they did show up a relapse?

He sat back down at the nurse's station and re-opened the computer, logging on to the imaging system and staring again at the X-ray. He took a deep, calming breath. Another hour, max, and the blood results would be back. This was killing him. If this was where loving someone got him, it was no wonder he'd avoided it all his life. It terrified him how much he cared. Hell, he'd almost punched a man because he cared so much. The anger that had consumed him when he'd walked into that cubicle and seen that drunken idiot pressed up against her, threatening her, had been overwhelming. His father had needed alcohol to give him the strength to lash out, but Dexter had been completely sober when he'd wanted to throw the man across the room and get him off Tilly.

It was caring about her that had done that. He cared about her, had wanted to protect her and nothing else had mattered...not even that he could have hurt someone or lost his job. Not even that it had turned him into his father—his biggest fear. He couldn't help that he cared—it was too late now not to let that happen—but he didn't have to let it go any further, did he?

Tilly deserved much more than he could offer her. Yes, being with her had changed him...a little. He'd been able to open up a little—relax more, run into the sea and dance and laugh in the rain. But, underneath, he was still Dexter Stevens—still lacking the emotional intelligence that came to her so naturally; still unable to allow himself to feel. Tilly needed more than that. He couldn't offer romance and roses and open discussions about emotions. She'd got the measure of him straight away—he was an antisocial, buttoned-up loner. A Grinch. And she deserved better. He'd only drag her down.

And he really didn't want to be in love.

COLETTE COOPER 207

He finished reviewing the X-ray and called to Mark, who was passing.

'Your patient who fell off the horse?'

'Oh, yes?' replied Mark. 'Any damage?'

'Supracondylar fracture of the right humerus,' said Dexter. 'Can you ask the orthos to see him? He'll probably need to go to Theatre.'

'Will do, boss,' replied Mark. 'Thanks.'

Dexter glanced at the time. It had been an hour. Tilly's results could be back. Resting his elbows on the desk, he dropped his head on his hands.

Dared he hope?

He logged onto the pathology reporting system and selected her name from the patient listing: moment of truth. He clicked on the report and a sea of black figures filled the screen. His eyes scanned them quickly.

Red cells normal.

White cells normal.

Platelets normal.

His head fell back and he screwed shut his eyes.

It wasn't his usual reaction to receiving blood results for patients.

He had to go and tell her.

He knocked on her office door. There was no answer. He knocked again, frowning. She hadn't gone and seen patients again, had she?

'Tilly? Are you in there?'

The door opened and Tilly stood looking at him, her amethyst eyes almost wary and without any of their usual sparkle. His heart broke for the anguish she must be going through. He stepped inside, closing the door behind him, turning to her and smiling. A flare of hope flamed in her eyes as she drew in a breath.

'You're fine, Tilly. Your bloods are perfectly normal.'

No words could have been sweeter to say to her. But then came words that stilled his soaring heart...

'I can go to Australia!'

She leapt at him, throwing her arms around him.

He hugged her and she buried her head into his neck.

'I'm so pleased, Tilly,' he whispered, as his heart sang for her and cracked for himself all in the same moment.

This must be what it felt like. He'd been lying to himself.

He did love her.

And it hurt—just as he'd always known it would.

CHAPTER EIGHTEEN

'STAY RIGHT WHERE you are,' said Dexter as Tilly threw back the duvet to get out of bed.

'I was going to pop some croissants into the air fryer—a day-off treat and a celebration of my perfect blood results,' she replied.

'I'll do it.' He was already halfway across the room.

Tilly snuggled back beneath the duvet, smiling, but then noticed her laptop on the chest of drawers. She had to send the email.

Dexter clattered about in his kitchen. 'Tilly?'

'Hello?'

'How many minutes do you put them in for?'

Her smile widened. 'Ten minutes, you domestic god, you.'

She'd never met anyone who melted her heart as he did, or whose eyes she could gaze into for ever. Who, even though he could be a monosyllabic grumpy bear, made her smile more than anyone else did. And he'd been exactly what she'd needed as she'd waited for her blood results. They'd grown so close and shared so much now. Did leaving him to follow her dream make sense any more?

Australia represented freedom. No one there knew of her cancer. No one would wrap her in cotton wool or treat her like precious china, liable to break at any moment. She could have a fresh start, a new beginning, where she would be judged for who she was now and not because she'd had leukaemia in the past. The slate would be wiped clean and the thought of that filled her soul with optimism, energy and hope.

If Dexter loved her and wanted her to stay, what would she do? The thought he might love her was joyful and terrifying in equal measure.

Australia was risk-free…a bright new start. But Dexter could hurt her all over again, as Lachlan had. Lachlan had told her he'd loved her, over and over, and he'd still hurt her in the end. Even people who said they loved you could hurt you, and Dexter had never even hinted that he had any feelings like that for her. He'd been the rock she'd needed him to be when she'd told him about her leukaemia. He'd stayed by her side, supporting her, cajoling her, even cooking for her. He hadn't run a million miles away.

But they were only work colleagues—friends with benefits at a push. He wasn't prepared to be more than that. Dexter had been supportive of a friend in need, but would he have been as supportive if they'd been more to each other? Would he have baulked at the pressure and responsibility of that, as Lachlan had?

The red flag still waved a warning she couldn't ignore. Yes, she'd got to know a little of the Dexter underneath the icy-cool exterior, but she still had doubts. He still kept secrets. He could still close himself down when he wanted to. And he didn't love her. He'd never said the words. Although, she'd never told him either. Maybe she should. Maybe she should tell him exactly how she felt—see where she stood.

'Ta-da!' Dexter stood in the doorway to the bedroom wearing nothing but a kitchen apron and holding aloft a tray of freshly baked croissants. 'Coffee to follow.'

He placed the tray on the bed and turned around, pausing only to look over his shoulder and give her the sexiest wink as she flicked her eyes from his perfect ass back to see it. He disappeared again, returning with two mugs of steaming coffee and placed them on the bedside tables.

'Perfect,' said Tilly, sitting up against her pillows with the duvet pulled up in front of her. She reached for her coffee, taking a sip and placing it back down. This had to be done and it had to be done now. She needed to know how he felt about her.

'You were right—you can cook. Lasagne yesterday, fresh croissants today... I think I'm in love with you.'

He grinned. 'With my cooking, you mean. I told you I wasn't bad.'

Her heart hammered. 'Not with your cooking, Dexter,' she replied, gazing into eyes she wanted to lose herself in. 'With you.'

He stared at her and she was certain he paled.

He swallowed, sitting up straighter. 'I'm not sure I understand.' He spoke slowly, as though carefully choosing his words.

He was going to run, but she had to know. Deep breath...

212 WEDDING FLING TO FOREVER

'I love you, Dexter.'

His lips parted, as though he was going to speak, but he clamped them shut, staring at her blankly, his mug of coffee suspended in mid-air halfway to his mouth.

The air left his lungs.

He couldn't think. Every single thought that had ever been in his head, every single word in his vocabulary, vanished. He carefully placed the mug back down on the bedside table, not trusting himself to perform that simple action without spilling it.

She loved him?

Helena had said that too. But he'd spent his life avoiding sweeping, grand, trouble-making emotions like love. How was he meant to respond?

'But I can see it's not reciprocated, so...'

He could only watch her as she reached for her bath robe and pulled it on.

But it *was* reciprocated.

It had been hell waiting for her blood results—it had been worse that she'd been so full of joy that she could go to Australia. Because it would mean losing her in a different way.

Which meant that he loved her.

So tell her.

But he was paralysed. It was as though someone had slapped him...hard.

'Wait, Tilly, where are you going?'

'To get a shower.'

He ran his fingers through his hair.

'Tilly, wait, please…we need to talk.'

He didn't want this. And he did.

Life was far easier the way he'd been living it since Helena. Doing his job at the hospital and at Battersea Dogs' and Cats' Home and looking after the animals, making a difference to people's lives—saving them, sometimes—was all he'd needed. Since Helena, everyone had been kept carefully at arm's length; his world had been ordered, calm and simple. There'd been no bumps or obstacles…at least, not ones that hadn't been easily sorted out by following the correct protocols or having the right knowledge.

Tilly sat back down on the bed, her bathnrobe wrapped tightly around her.

But love had a whole different set of rules. And he had no idea what they were.

It had been one thing to admit to *himself* that he loved Tilly—that had been done covertly, inside his own head, without having to divulge it to anyone else. But there was no way he could admit it out loud—that would make it too real. And making it real scared the living daylights out of him. He didn't trust love—it had always let him down. Love had two sides to it—it could fill a person with hope but they always had to be ready to run from it before the inevitable damage occurred. It sent rational thinking and decision-making hurtling out into oblivion. It made a person run into the North Sea fully clothed, threaten people with violence…risk a livelihood.

But he did love her. And he couldn't hurt her.

'I don't—' he began.

214 WEDDING FLING TO FOREVER

'Do relationships?' cut in Tilly, her chin held high. 'Yes, I remember you saying that. I just wondered if perhaps we'd moved on. Obviously not.'

'Tilly, I can't offer you what you're looking for. I'm not that person.'

She laughed thinly. 'That's such an "it's not you, it's me" comment, Dexter.'

'It's true.'

She held up her hand, not looking at him as she reached for her laptop.

'What are you doing?'

'Sending an email,' she replied.

'To the agency?'

'Yes.'

'To confirm your start date?'

'Yes.'

He closed his eyes tightly, screwing them shut as he spoke the word he knew he had to…for her sake. She deserved better than anything he could offer her.

'Good.'

She stopped tapping the keyboard and swung round to face him, the sparkle he loved so much missing.

'Yes,' she said quietly, before continuing.

'It's your dream.' He wasn't about to take that away from her.

'It is.'

'You can't not go.' He was just being logical. She needed this. She needed to make her dream come true, prove her independence. He wanted that for her…more than he could give her.

But she loved him.

Was this what love was—two people hurting? Two people who cared about each other breaking each other's hearts?

He didn't want that. He didn't want her to be hurt. He wanted her to be happy. But he had hurt her and he hated that.

She was better off without him—look what he'd done to her. It was best she went, best she made that new life for herself she dreamed about. Nothing he could give her could match that.

'That's not true,' she replied, turning to him and looking into his eyes, melting his heart with the intensity of her gaze. 'I don't have to go—if I had a reason to stay.'

Was *he* the reason she'd stay? If he told her he loved her, would that mean she wouldn't go?

The words were on his lips. But he couldn't say them. He'd never been able to say them. Helena had screamed at him to tell her he loved her, but he hadn't been able to, and it had cost him their relationship.

Was that happening all over again? There was a choice laid out in front of him, two paths: loving Tilly or holding on to the life he knew…secure behind the walls he'd built around himself.

So, choose: logical or illogical.

What he said next would determine both their futures. It was huge. And being logical was the only way to deal with making huge, important decisions.

'It's your dream…you have to go. I can't offer you anything more, Tilly.'

Her gaze didn't falter. He didn't want to look away. She was the warm fire he'd come home to in a cold winter; the safe harbour after battling through a storm. But she challenged him, too. He'd lost some of the control he'd had in his life. He'd succumbed to feelings he'd never wanted. He was losing his grip on everything he believed in…because that was what falling in love did to people.

'I know you struggle with expressing your feelings, Dexter. I get that, after what you went through as a child, you want to stay in control…never get hurt again. I'm sorry you went through that but—'

'Don't feel sorry for me.' He didn't want her pity. He didn't want reminding of a past he'd rather forget. He'd told her too much already; given away painful secrets he should have kept hidden.

He dragged on his boxer shorts and jeans. The child he'd once been was forgotten—the memories had been packed away in a box in his head, a box that had been locked shut, never to be opened. The only way it could stay locked was if he never thought about it. If any thoughts showed signs of bubbling to the surface, he pushed them back down before they could be fully formed. But Tilly kept trying to prise those thoughts and feelings out of him. This was why he'd never let anyone get close.

'It clearly still affects you, Dexter.'

He pulled his T-shirt over his head. He wasn't going to think about this—he wasn't going to open that box again. He shouldn't have told her what he'd already told her about his past. Why had he?

Because he'd recklessly allowed himself to feel something for her—to care about her, to love her. And love made people think and do things without logic; without taking a step back, looking at the situation and coming to a rational conclusion.

And that wasn't him. He was taking a step back now, looking at the situation…and saw that it was hurting both of them.

'It doesn't affect me any more, Tilly—it really doesn't—and if you think that you don't know me at all.'

A shaft of morning sunshine lay across her, making her ebony hair shine.

'I know you hide behind that cool, hard-edged exterior to try to prevent anything or anyone reaching you. And I know that's not really who you are, because I've seen what's beneath all that armour you wear, behind the thick stone wall you've built around yourself. I've seen the real Dexter, and he's still cowering in a corner, trying not to get hurt again. You don't need to do that any more.'

He stared at her, his mind racing, struggling to put his thoughts into any kind of order.

Was that what she thought of him? That he was still a terrified young boy?

He'd dealt with all that…moved on. He could handle it all—everything that had happened to him. He wasn't a young child any more, terrified about what would happen to him next—one minute hating his

218   WEDDING FLING TO FOREVER

father with every atom of his being, the next desperately finding ways to hide his bruises so he wasn't taken into care. He was an adult now, and fully in control of what happened in his life. And he was going to take control of this.

She didn't move, not an inch. Her eyes held his.

He dragged in a breath. He needed to get this over with...so that they could both move on. Tilly deserved so much more than he could offer. Hell, he was in love with her, and was so screwed up he couldn't even tell her. Tilly needed fun and freedom, and a man who'd give that to her. She needed the romance...the happy-ever-after. He couldn't give her those things. She was right about him: he *was* a Grinch. He'd crush her beautiful spirit.

And there was no way on earth he was ever going to allow that to happen. He'd spent his entire life fighting to protect himself in one way or another, then she'd come along and now his barricade lay broken...in pieces.

She'd got him to open up.

She'd shown him how to let go.

It had been exhilarating. And terrifying.

If this was what love was, he'd been right to steer well clear of it.

'I told you I don't do relationships, Tilly. You should send that email.' He picked up his phone and slipped it into his pocket, but he didn't want to go, and stood looking at her a moment longer. At the woman who'd got under his skin so much that he'd taken his eye of the ball and allowed himself to feel something for her, to care too much about her…to fall in love with her.

'I promised I'd help out at Battersea this morning.'

That was why it was so hard to walk away now. But it was also why the words that told her to leave slipped so easily from his mouth, even though saying them was the hardest thing he'd ever done. Because it was the right thing to do. The logical thing.

'Are you telling me it's over, Dexter?'

The sunlight fell on her hair. He wanted to touch it. He wanted to look into her eyes for the rest of eternity. But her eyes were misted and it killed him to see what he'd done to her. He needed to leave.

'Send the email. I can't love you, Tilly.'

She needed her adventure…she didn't need him. He was everything she didn't need in her life.

And *he* needed to take back control of his feelings.

CHAPTER NINETEEN

'YOU OKAY THIS MORNING, TILLY?' It was Mark, who'd pulled up a chair beside her at the nurse's station. 'You seem a bit quiet.'

'Just thinking how much I'll miss this place,' she replied, managing a smile. She'd sent the email the day that Dexter had thrown her feelings for him back in her face, some two weeks ago now. They'd kept their distance from each other since, Tilly changing her shifts to avoid him as much as possible. When they'd had to work together on a patient, they'd remained professionally polite, but nothing more. The day she'd told him she loved him, and he'd reacted by telling her he didn't love her back, hadn't been mentioned.

'You must be so excited too, though—you've wanted this for such a long time and now and it's about to happen. I'm sure you won't miss us for long, not when you can finish a shift and be on Bondi beach within minutes. We'll miss you, though.' He touched her arm and smiled a sorrowful smile.

'Thanks, Mark—I'm definitely looking forward to beach life. But right now...' she pointed to the electronic patient board '... I need to sort out Mr Parkes in cubicle five.'

She heard Dexter's voice in one of the cubicles as she passed. After today, she'd never hear it again, and she simply had to accept that. Just as she had to accept that he didn't love her.

'Morning, Mr Parkes; my name's Tilly and I'm one of the nurses. So, what's brought you in today?'

She'd told Dexter she loved him and he hadn't wanted to hear it. The words had made him want to run a thousand miles away...or make him want to tell her to put thousands of miles between them. He was doing much as Lachlan had done, except he hadn't ended it because of her leukaemia—he'd ended it because he didn't love her. She was the one who was leaving, but it was Dexter who'd wanted her to. He'd been honest with her from the start—he didn't do relationships or romance; he didn't believe in happy-ever-afters. He'd told her he couldn't offer her more. But, for some stupid reason, she'd thought that maybe he'd changed.

'So, if you're happy,' she said to the patient, 'I'm going to start the antibiotics intravenously and then you'll be able to carry on with them by mouth. Is that okay?'

The rest of the day continued as the days in Trafalgar A&E always did. The only difference was that now she knew that Dexter didn't want her, and her heart was broken. But she still had her dream and she was going to go out there and live it.

The days and weeks in Trafalgar A&E continued as they always did. The only difference was that Tilly wasn't there. And life just wasn't the same without her. He glanced at a photo someone had

printed out and pinned to one of the notice boards—
of Tilly with her team on the sea in a dragon boat,
in the Australian sunshine. She was laughing. She
looked happy. He looked away, his heart swelling
with pride for her. She'd made it happen—she was
living her dream.

And he'd been an idiot.

'Your results are back, Mr Seabridge,' said Dexter, standing at the bottom of the trolley on which
his patient lay.

'What's the verdict, Doc?'

'Well, the sudden onset of flank pain radiating
inferiolaterally...' The patient's eyes were narrowed
in concentration as he listened. Dexter stopped and
thought for a moment. 'You have a kidney stone.'

'I thought you were going all technical on me
there for a minute,' said Daniel Seabridge, grinning,
'I haven't been to medical school, you know.'

Tilly. It was Tilly who'd shown him how to be a
better doctor. It was Tilly who'd shown him how
to be a better human being—how to relax; how to
enjoy life more. She'd shown him how to run barefoot in the sand; how to run hand in hand through
the rain; how to care and how to fall in love.

'I've spoken to one of the specialist kidney doctors and they're going to come along and see you as
soon as they can. Have you any questions?'

'Not at the minute, Doc, thanks.'

'See you later,' said Dexter, pushing the curtain
aside and returning to the nurse's station to write
up his notes.

Mark sat a couple of seats away; Anika scurried past with a trolley laden with equipment; Pearl pointed, giving directions to the fracture clinic to a mum with a young child who had his arm in a plaster, decorated with cartoon characters. Everything was as it always had been—everything was the same.

Except for him. He wasn't the same. He hadn't been the same since the day Tilly Clover had turned up in his department and rocked his entire world.

And he would never be the same. Because she'd changed him. And, stupidly, he hadn't seen it until it was too late.

She'd said she loved him. And he hadn't known how to respond.

Had losing Helena taught him nothing? He'd spent his entire life avoiding emotion, protecting himself from the pain and humiliation of caring and having it thrown back in his face. He'd been so terrified of discovering he was the same as his angry, violent father that he'd fought against feeling anything deeper than respect for other people.

But he hadn't banked on Tilly dancing into his life and filling it with warmth, joy and the possibility of genuine happiness. He hadn't been able to accept her love for him was real. All he'd seen was the fear that ran underneath loving someone.

He'd loved her for a long time. He knew that now. If he'd stopped to think for a moment instead of fighting against it, he would have realised that, even though he'd fallen in love, nothing bad had happened as a result.

The world hadn't ended. He hadn't turned into his father—in fact, quite the opposite. The world had become a better place—he'd been able to run barefoot in the sand and headlong into the sea fully clothed. And, when pushed to the limit, needing to defend Tilly from a violent man in A&E, he'd controlled his understandable anger and dealt with the situation as a professional.

He'd fallen in love with Tilly and he'd never been happier.

And then, he'd thrown it all away. Because he'd been afraid to say the words he should have said to her a long time ago—that he loved her too. The barricades he'd put up to protect himself from getting hurt had been counterproductive. They hadn't protected him at all. They'd prevented him from being able to accept the only happiness he'd ever had the chance of.

Did he want to regret that for the rest of his life? If he didn't, there was only one thing to do—he had to find her and he had to say the words he'd never said to anyone.

CHAPTER TWENTY

TILLY SAT ON the beach towel watching the surfers ride the waves as the late-afternoon sun warmed her skin and the soft sand trickled through her fingers. Her long-held, far-off dream was now her reality and she closed her eyes behind her sunglasses, lifting her face to the sky and listening to the waves pounding the beach. A cool shadow fell over her and she tentatively opened one eye. There had been no clouds in the sky when she'd last looked.

A dark figure towered over her, standing at her feet and wearing blue swimming shorts.

She froze. She'd know that toned torso anywhere. *Dexter.*

Lifting herself to a sitting position, she took off her sunglasses. It *was* him.

'What on earth…?' But even if she *had* known what she was going to say next, she didn't have the chance to say the words. Dexter dropped to his knees in the sand beside her.

'I miss you.'

It would have been so easy to look into those deep blue, earnest eyes and lose herself. She replaced her sunglasses.

'You came halfway across the world to tell me that?'

'And other things.'

'What other things?'

'I...'

She stared at him. *He missed her*—but it had taken him three months to realise?

'Are you here on a conference or something?' He hadn't come all this way just to see her, surely, not after he'd told her to go?

'No, I came to find you.'

Her heart rate picked up. Damn that he still had that effect on her... 'Why?'

'Because I...miss you.'

'You're the one who told me to leave.' Her voice was quiet. It was still hard to acknowledge that he'd rejected her so coldly; hard to say the words. 'You told me you didn't want a relationship.'

'I was stupid.'

'You're still a man of few words, I see.'

A smile played at the corners of his mouth.

'You know me so well.'

'Knew,' she corrected. 'Or thought I did.'

'You know me better than anyone.'

'You kept so much hidden.'

'You should have seen me before you came along.'

'Meaning what?' She knew she sounded a little terse, and didn't mean to, but suddenly seeing him again after all this time was a little overwhelming, to say the least.

'I was a Grinch.' He smiled—a tentative smile, almost shy, as though he wasn't sure whether it was appropriate or not, but it made his dark blue eyes sparkle just the same. And it made her want to gaze into them.

COLETTE COOPER 227

'And now you're not?'

He dropped his gaze for a moment before lifting his eyes and fixing her with them again. 'Less so.'

She raised an eyebrow at him.

'You look well,' he said. 'Happy.'

'I am happy.' She opened her arms wide, looking at the view before them. 'Who wouldn't be, with all of this?'

'I'm not. Not without you.'

Her heart began to thump harder.

He'd flown across the world to tell her this. Dexter—king of no emotion...

But he'd rejected her. She'd told him she loved him, and he'd told her to leave. She'd been hurt and humiliated...she still was.

And she still thought about him. Too much. Even being thousands of miles apart hadn't stopped that.

But it didn't matter. He didn't love her. He said he'd missed her—not that he loved her. She wasn't angry with him. It had been her decision to begin a relationship with the most unsuitable man in the world—she only had herself to blame.

'Tilly, I...' He glanced around the beach. It was late afternoon and busy with people. A volleyball game was in full swing; couples were walking along the water's edge; children were paddling; a family was having a picnic just a few feet away. He fixed his gaze back on her and she realised that she knew him well enough to see that he was struggling.

He sighed and ran his fingers through his dark hair. 'I've never said this before.' He lowered his head and a lock of hair fell forward again, covering his eyes.

'What can be so bad that you can't say the words?' She spoke softly, gently, dipping her head to see his face.

He lifted his eyes but his head remained bent. His fingers played with the sand beneath them. And then his jaw hardened, his chin lifted and he drew in a long breath.

'It's nothing bad; it's just alien to me. But I've flown over ten thousand miles to tell you this, and I'm damn sure I'm going to make sure you hear me.'

Tilly watched him as he rose slowly to his feet. She sat up and he looked down at her, his feet planted solidly, his chin high, shoulders back. His eyes never left hers.

'I've never said this to anyone before, Tilly, and I never expected that I would, but you've changed that. I was stupid to let you walk away without me and I've regretted it every moment since. Life isn't the same without you. If you've moved on and don't want me around, I understand that, but I've come here to tell you one thing…'

Her head was scrambled; a million thoughts ran around and crashed into each other. 'Yes?' Her voice was soft, urging him to speak, to say the words he'd come here to say. Dared she hope?

He drew in a breath.

'I… I believe I may have misled you into thinking that I have no feelings for you.'

She stared at him and he dropped his gaze, stuffing his hands into his pockets before looking back at her sheepishly.

'This is so you, Dexter.'

He nodded. 'You know me.'

And she still loved him. She loved him for how deeply caring he was, as well as for all the awkwardness when it came to showing his feelings.

'I do,' she replied, conceding a smile.

His jaw relaxed and his face softened.

'I love you, Tilly.'

It was little more than a whisper, but she heard him, and all she could do was stare at him as she tried to remember how to breathe.

'I don't think she heard you, mate.' It was the father of the picnicking family a short distance away. 'You might need to tell her again.'

The mum sat looking at them, her hands clasped together at her chest and smiling with delight. She spoke softly to Dexter. 'Go on, tell her again, love—make sure she hears you.'

Dexter looked back at Tilly and smiled…a wide, genuine, suddenly confident smile that lit up his deep blue eyes, making them sparkle. He opened his arms wide.

'I love you, Tilly Clover.'

And this time she heard him say the words loudly, clearly and confidently. There was a small round of applause from the picnicking family but Tilly only had eyes for Dexter. She got to her feet and stood before him, smiling up into his beautiful, genuine blue eyes.

'Let's go for a walk.' She picked up the beach towel, rolling it and slotting it into her bag. They headed for the shoreline, where they walked in silence along the beach on the edge of the cool, clear blue water that lapped at their feet.

This was her dream: living in Australia; having an amazing job; strolling along the beach with the sun warming her skin; listening to the rhythmic crashing of the waves. And she'd been fine. If she could have added anything extra, it would have been to have all that and a wonderful, thoughtful, genuine, kind and maybe incredibly handsome man beside her too.

And here she was, with all she'd dreamed of and the cherry on top: Dexter.

He loved her. He'd travelled all the way to Australia to tell her, to say the words he'd never said before and never thought he'd ever say to anyone.

But he'd said them to *her*.

'Say something,' he said as she dropped her bag on the sand in a quiet little cove further along the beach. 'Please...even if it's to tell me to go back to London and never darken your doorstep again.'

'I'd never tell you that.'

'You have every reason to—I was an idiot. I qualified it in my head by telling myself that I was protecting you.'

'From what?'

'From me.'

She frowned. 'I don't need protecting from you.

I don't need protecting at all—that's what coming here is all about. I've been fine.'

Dexter held up his hands. 'No, not in that way. Look at you—you've achieved what you wanted to and I'm so proud of you. What I meant was that I wanted more for you.'

'In what way?'

He shrugged.

'We're two very different people, Tilly. You're full of fun and sparkle and I'm…well…the proverbial Grinch.'

'But yin and yang balance each other. One can't exist without the other.'

'And I can't offer you romance.'

A slow smile shaped her lips. 'You've flown ten thousand miles to find me, and you told me you love me in front of a beach full of Australians…and you say you don't do romance?'

'Is that romantic?'

She grinned.

'It's not a bad attempt, Dexter.'

He reached for her fingers, touching them lightly.

'I'm really rubbish at emotional stuff.'

She pursed her lips thoughtfully. 'You're learning, though.'

'I've been a blundering idiot, so terrified of allowing love to ruin my carefully controlled world that I ruined it myself by denying it. I've never trusted love, Tilly. I've protected my cold heart from ever feeling it because I thought letting it in was too much of a risk. I didn't want my castle walls knocked down. Have I left it too late to hope that what you said to me hasn't long since died away?'

Tilly held onto his fingers, drawing him towards her.

'It's not too late, Dexter. I still love you…that hasn't changed.'

He took hold of her other hand and, grasping them both, pulled her towards him, dipping his head as she smiled up at him, and pressed his lips to hers. A lifetime had passed since he'd last crushed his lips to hers; it seemed for ever since she'd been in the warm embrace of his strong arms.

'If you'll have me, Tilly, I'd love to explore the option of applying for a visa.'

'For Australia?'

'I've already spoken to my old colleague who moved over here, and he's given me some really useful information.'

Her hand few to her mouth.

'Is that good shock or bad shock?' said Dexter, looking concerned.

He did love her. He loved her so much that he was prepared to move to the other side of the world for her and leave the job that meant everything to him.

'Good shock. And you say you're not romantic?'

'Is that romantic too?'

She smiled. 'I think my yin and your yang have a very good chance of being very good together, Dexter. I'd love you to apply for a visa.'

And the smile playing at the corners of his lips blossomed into the widest grin she'd ever seen.

'I love you, Tilly Clover.'
And, suddenly, every wonderful dream about her future that she'd ever had became very, very real.

EPILOGUE

'LADIES AND GENTS,' said the compere in a broad Australian accent. 'Can I have your attention, please? The bride and groom are about to have their first dance.'

A cheer and round of applause went up in the ballroom. The harbourside hotel in Sydney was perfectly placed for amazing views of the city, the Opera House and the famous harbour bridge. Dexter and Tilly had relaxed on the rooftop terrace there many times in the last year, and it had become one of their favourite places in the city. But they were there now for the wedding of two of their colleagues from Bondi A&E.

Tilly smiled and waved at Isla, catching her eye as she was led to the dance floor by Taylor, her new husband.

'They look so happy,' she said, squeezing Dexter's hand as they stood on the edge of the dance floor watching the newlyweds. He didn't hate parties any more. Living in Australia meant they were invited to gatherings all the time—'barbies' in people's back gardens were almost obligatory—and with Tilly's support he'd begun to relax. He now actively enjoyed hosting a get-together and sizzling sausages and burgers in the sunshine for friends.

'They do,' agreed Dexter. 'I suppose you're going to want to join them on that dance floor any second?' He looked down at her, a question arching his brow.

'Of course,' she replied, grinning at him. 'You can show off your waltz moves.'

'Calling my moves "a waltz" is a bit of a stretch… I can sway a little, that's all.'

'Anyone who'd like to join the bride and groom, please make your way onto the dance floor,' called the compere.

Tilly pulled Dexter's hand and he groaned.

'Don't be a party pooper, Dexter Stevens,' she chided. She wanted to be held by him, and feel close to him, one last time before she told him.

'Wouldn't dream of it,' he replied, placing one hand on her waist, the other hand intertwined with her fingers. He moved his feet, swaying gently to the music, as they had many times at their home in Bondi.

Dexter's visa had come through quickly because of his qualifications, experience and the vacancies at the hospital, and he'd joined Tilly at the house she'd been renting near the beach. He'd settled into his role as consultant quickly and, like Tilly, loved the fact they could be at the beach within minutes of finishing work. He and Tilly had been open from the start about their relationship and had been warmly welcomed, very quickly feeling loved and respected enormously by the team.

The song ended and everyone applauded before the DJ began playing a more upbeat song, and Dexter frowned at Tilly as she began to dance.

236   WEDDING FLING TO FOREVER

'I'll sit this one out.'

Tilly smiled at him. She'd coaxed him into dancing but he was really only comfortable doing so when they were alone.

'Shall we go up onto the roof terrace...watch the sunset over the harbour?'

She had something to tell him and telling him in this very special place overlooking the city they'd come to love seemed perfect. She and Dexter had been so happy together over the last year. Australia was everything she'd hoped for and more. They'd learnt to surf; Dexter had joined her dragon-boat racing team; they were picking up 'the lingo' and had even been told by Aussie friends that their barbie skills were almost as good as the locals.

'Sounds like a much better idea,' said Dexter, smiling. 'In fact, I was about to suggest it myself.'

The lights on Sydney Opera House glowed against the darkening sky and the twinkling water of the harbour below. Everyone else was downstairs in the ballroom, partying with the newlyweds. The rooftop garden was beautifully planted with exotically scented, brightly coloured flowers, lit softly with fairy lights and dotted with benches and coloured bean bags.

The timing was perfect. But, even though she knew Dexter now better than she'd known anyone else, there remained the tiny niggle of concern about his reaction to what she was about to tell him. He wasn't Lachlan, but her news was pretty momentous, and the chance that he might want to run most definitely came with it. But he loved her. He'd followed her to the other side of the world, and he told her he loved her every single day.

'I don't think I'll ever tire of this view,' he said, standing behind Tilly, his arms around her waist, his chin resting lightly on the top of her head.

'Me neither.' She turned to face him and he kept hold of her, planting a kiss on her forehead. 'Let me give you a reason to remember this view for ever, Dexter...to remember this night for ever.'

Dexter smiled and her insides melted, as they always did when he smiled at her.

'I was going to say the same thing to you.'

'Really?'

'Really...it's why I wanted to come up here.'

'Not just because of the wedding?'

'Not to get away from the wedding particularly, no, but the wedding is partly the reason.'

'How so?'

'Weddings make people do all sorts of crazy, romantic things, don't they?'

'Like what?'

Dexter let go of her waist but held onto her hands.

'I love this city and I love you, Tilly. And up here, in this special place under the stars, I wanted to ask you...'

He reached into his trouser pocket and pulled out a small white box, opening it to reveal a white-gold ring set with diamonds and amethysts. 'If you would do me the honour of becoming my wife.'

Tilly looked from the ring to his face and his cobalt eyes which were full of love…for her…and her heart swelled to the point she thought it would burst. She nodded, smiling, unable to speak.

He cocked his head to one side, looking at her. 'Is that a yes?'

'It's a yes, Dexter.'

Taking the ring from the box, he pushed it gently onto her finger.

'It's beautiful, Dexter; thank you.'

And, when she looked back up into the eyes she could lose herself in for ever, they were misted with genuine love. And in that moment she knew that the news she'd been about to tell him—that they were expecting a baby—wasn't going to make him want to run… If it was possible, it was going to bring them even closer together than they already were.

* * * * *

*If you enjoyed this story,
check out this other great read from
Colette Cooper*

Nurse's Twin Baby Surprise

Available now!

Get up to 4 Free Books!

We'll send you 2 free books from each series you try
PLUS a free Mystery Gift.

Both the **Harlequin Presents** and **Harlequin Medical Romance** series
feature exciting stories of passion and drama.

YES! Please send me 2 FREE novels from Harlequin Presents or Harlequin Medical Romance and my FREE gift (gift is worth about $10 retail). After receiving them, if I don't wish to receive any more books, I can return the shipping statement marked "cancel." If I don't cancel, I will receive 6 brand-new larger-print novels every month and be billed just $7.19 each in the U.S., or $7.99 each in Canada, or 4 brand-new Harlequin Medical Romance Larger-Print books every month and be billed just $7.19 each in the U.S. or $7.99 each in Canada, a savings of 20% off the cover price. It's quite a bargain! Shipping and handling is just 50¢ per book in the U.S. and $1.25 per book in Canada.* I understand that accepting the 2 free books and gift places me under no obligation to buy anything. I can always return a shipment and cancel at any time. The free books and gift are mine to keep no matter what I decide.

Choose one:
- ☐ **Harlequin Presents Larger-Print** (176/376 BPA G36Y)
- ☐ **Harlequin Medical Romance** (171/371 BPA G36Y)
- ☐ **Or Try Both!** (176/376 & 171/371 BPA G36Z)

Name (please print)

Address   Apt. #

City   State/Province   Zip/Postal Code

Email: Please check this box ☐ if you would like to receive newsletters and promotional emails from Harlequin Enterprises ULC and its affiliates. You can unsubscribe anytime.

Mail to the **Harlequin Reader Service:**
IN U.S.A.: P.O. Box 1341, Buffalo, NY 14240-8531
IN CANADA: P.O. Box 603, Fort Erie, Ontario L2A 5X3

Want to explore our other series or interested in ebooks? Visit www.ReaderService.com or call 1-800-873-8635.

---

*Terms and prices subject to change without notice. Prices do not include sales taxes, which will be charged (if applicable) based on your state or country of residence. Canadian residents will be charged applicable taxes. Offer not valid in Quebec. This offer is limited to one order per household. Books received may not be as shown. Not valid for current subscribers to the Harlequin Presents or Harlequin Medical Romance series. All orders subject to approval. Credit or debit balances in a customer's account(s) may be offset by any other outstanding balance owed by or to the customer. Please allow 4 to 6 weeks for delivery. Offer available while quantities last.

Your Privacy—Your information is being collected by Harlequin Enterprises ULC, operating as Harlequin Reader Service. For a complete summary of the information we collect, how we use this information and to whom it is disclosed, please visit our privacy notice located at https://corporate.harlequin.com/privacy-notice. Notice to California Residents – Under California law, you have specific rights to control and access your data. For more information on these rights and how to exercise them, visit https://corporate.harlequin.com/california-privacy. For additional information for residents of other U.S. states that provide their residents with certain rights with respect to personal data, visit https://corporate.harlequin.com/other-state-residents-privacy-rights/.

HPHM25